THE COURTYARD CONUNDRUM

A WEAL & WOE BOOKSHOP WITCH MYSTERY

CATE MARTIN

Cover design by Shezaad Sudar.

Ratatoskr Press logo by Aidan Vincent Kise.

ISBN 978-1-958606-78-0

❀ Created with Vellum

CHAPTER

ONE

Autumn has always been my favorite time of the year, and October is peak autumn.

And, as I quickly discovered this particular October, the magical neighborhood known as the Square hidden in the St. Anthony area of Minneapolis—the part of the world I had made my home—did autumn really, really well.

Because while the Square was closed in on all four sides by shops on the ground floor and two levels of apartment buildings above, the heart of its space was all nature. And while the hedge maze remained as vibrantly green as ever, the orchard on the other half of the open plaza was a riot of fall colors. The sun may hang lower in the southern sky, but when it hits those trees, it lights up all those leaves in shades of gold, amber and scarlet like nature's own stained glass.

Not to mention the sweet smell of apples still hangs in the air like the ghost of harvests past, mingling with the fresh, dry smell of fallen leaves that rises up with every step under the limbs of those trees.

So when the weather got cooler, and the nights got longer, and the dinners I shared with my uncles suddenly featured lots of pumpkin soup, pumpkin curry, and pumpkin ravioli, I should've been in heaven.

But I wasn't. I was just... numb.

Granted, September had been a rough month for me, even before my mother had appeared out of nowhere in my bedroom and drained me of nearly every last bit of my precious magic. Still, that had been weeks ago.

And from a prosaic—by which I mean nonmagical—point of view, I had completely recovered. I could make it through an entire day now without needing a nap or two to get my strength back. I was back to helping out in my uncles' bookshop even with the more strenuous stuff, like hauling boxes of books up and down the seven flights of stairs.

But from a magical point of view, I was still completely drained.

Which really wasn't unusual for me. For as long as I could remember, I had always been drained of power. No matter where I was in the world, which magical academy I was struggling to perform in, my mother would always show up at some point, slinking into the darkness of my bedroom at night and slinking away again after leaving me a powerless husk.

For the longest time, I had thought those were all dreams.

For the longest time, I had no idea that I wasn't actually a witch with no magic. I was a witch who kept having her magic taken from her. By her own mother.

But after I'd come to the Square, my mother had stopped draining me. Not because she didn't still want to. No, it was because one of the first friends I had made after coming to the Square was Houdini. Houdini, who looked like a rat terrier chihuahua, but was actually a dragon hidden under layer after layer of protective magic.

He might look like a scrawny ten-pound ankle biter, but he could make you feel the whole size of him when he wanted to. He was still young, still a dragonet. But even young as he was, he was larger than four elephants. And he could loom with the force of all that dragon might.

Although, so far, he had only ever done it to protect me. He'd driven my mother away, more than once.

But in September, he had almost gotten there too late to save me. She had been drawing so much more power out of me than she ever had before. And I didn't think she intended to stop.

If Houdini hadn't come to my rescue, I might still be needing all those naps to get through the day.

Or, you know, worse.

But he *had* gotten there in time, and I had recovered. Everything except the magic that I was honestly more used to not having, and had never learned how to control.

So why was I still feeling so down? Why was even October, with all of its inherent charms, not lifting my spirits at all?

I had so much in my life now that I'd never had before. I had gone from not having any family besides my mostly absent mother to having a pair of loving uncles who took me in, gave me a home in their attic apartment overlooking that magic Square, and let me work in their even more magical bookshop.

And I had that bookshop, which loved me without words, giving me a little nook of my own on its fourth level overlooking the Minneapolis streets below. I had an immense study table with plenty of room for the stacks and stacks of books I had arranged in a system only I could understand, tracking every thread of my research into my own power and how it worked. And I had a comfy window seat, just perfect for curling up with a book before one of those inevitable naps overwhelmed me.

Sure, I had gained and then lost a twin brother in a breathtakingly short amount of time. And as angry as I was with him for his betrayal, I still ached at the loss.

But I also had friends. Besides Houdini, who never left my side, there were Audrey Mirken and her boyfriend Liam Kelly. If I didn't meet them every morning for a breakfast of tea and scones in Audrey's teashop before it opened for the day, they would come up to my bedroom to find me and make sure I was okay.

And then there was my boyfriend, Steph Underwood. As the apprentice to the Wizard who lived in the Tower at the far end of the Square, he had a ton of heavy responsibilities, not least of which was maintaining the spells that protected the Square. But even on his busiest of days, he made time to see me.

And to bring me more books. Because even though I worked in one of the largest magical bookshops in the world, there were always more books out there. Books in private libraries or obscure shops in hidden corners of other magical neighborhoods all throughout the world.

Books that might help me figure out how my magic worked.

But it wasn't so much the books themselves that I appreciated, although they were, of course, always welcome. No, it was more that by constantly finding more and more texts for me to search for clues about my power, it was like he was always silently reinforcing what he and the Wizard were also always flat out telling me.

I would get my power back. My mother had drained me, but not entirely. It would take time, but my power would return.

And something in those books just might help me learn how to master it before it grew beyond my ability to control again.

Because the thing is, the branch of magic that I was born to practice is the one sort of magic that is strictly forbidden by all the magic councils everywhere.

It's not necromancy. It's not mind control or the sorts of spells with effects like nuclear bombs. I mean, those are all technically *regulated*. But only one branch of magic is outright *banned*.

Chaos.

And all the actual books about chaos had been destroyed centuries ago. I almost got my hands on one lost copy of a book that probably wasn't even going to be helpful, but the man who possessed it set it and himself on fire rather than let me see it.

That's how powerful the forces are that don't want me learning how to use my own power.

But the Wizard helped me find a different way. Because while every mention of chaos magic had been purged from every book in existence, the censors had not been able to remove all the references to chaos magic that weren't labeled chaos magic.

Sometimes magic is described by its effects without ever being named. Perhaps the wizard who wrote the account didn't know what it was. Or perhaps he did, but he wisely avoided naming the forbidden thing.

Either way, there were books where chaos magic was explained. Only, given that they weren't labeled as such, those accounts were hard to find.

I mean, not every mention of an unknown magic is actually a mention of chaos magic. There's lots of unknown things in the world. As true as that is in the prosaic world, it's doubly so in the magic one.

And the further I got on my journey of research, the fewer things I found that felt to me like real chaos magic.

I had been attempting to learn more about my own power ever since I had learned just what it was. Which was only a few months ago, after a lifetime of assuming I was just a witch with no real power to speak of. The Wizard helped a lot, as did Steph.

But in the end, no one understood what that power felt like except me.

With the possible exception of my mother. But given that she had chosen not to be a presence in my life beyond turning up every few months to suck all my power away, I had never learned a single thing from her.

I guess I believed the power would come back. I mean, the Wizard swore he could sense it building back inside me already.

But I didn't sense it. I still felt so very empty inside. Like there was a hollow coldness in my core that no amount of pumpkin soup could ever fill or warm up.

Worse, the world around me felt empty, too. Like colors were muted, sounds were muffled, and everyone was so far away.

October was so far away.

I had been in this funk for more than a month, despite everyone bringing me whatever they could think of that would bring something bright and delightful into my life.

But what finally brought me out of it wasn't something someone did for me. It was something I decided to do for someone else.

I set all the books aside that were meant to help me master my still-missing chaos power, and I turned my attention to something else. A very different sort of spell.

In September, I had touched on the magic that had built the Square. I had used it at the time to write a spell for my friend Audrey to cast to grow a new room onto her tiny apartment. It had worked like a charm. She had ended up with a large sunny room all to herself, plus a secret garden she shared with all the other apartments on that side of the Square.

Steph had worked out that the Square was providing everyone with emergency exits out of the building, a fact that still stewed in the back of all our minds since we didn't know yet what the Square thought we might have to escape *from*.

But if I set that paranoia aside in the back of my mind and just focused on that garden, it was really a lovely place. The bookshop had a door that opened onto it, and while everyone liked to stroll through it and touch the plants or sit on its comfy benches, it still always felt like a secluded place. Even with others there too, you could be quietly alone there.

I had just been thinking of that spell one morning as I came down to my nook before heading to the teashop for breakfast and saw a fresh stack of books waiting for me at the end of my study table. Some of the books were familiar, but not from my chaos research.

I knew them from my structural magic research. And as I paged through them again, a fresh idea took shape inside my mind.

Which was how I ended up writing a spell that would bring the spirit of a shop to life.

Because shops have a structure defined by the Square, and

within the confines of that structure, they have an existence of sorts. Maybe not sentience per se—although I strongly suspected my uncles' bookshop was, in fact, sentient—but a unique presence that could be captured by a spell and given a physical, if only ghostly, form.

I freely admit I didn't think it through too much. That burst of energy, of feeling like there was something I could do, and it was something that would actually be a good thing, or at least a temporarily amusing thing, took me over.

But as soon as I had scribbled down a draft of a spell, I knew I had to try it out.

Or, rather, get my friend Audrey to try it out.

I couldn't wait to see her face when she realized just what my new spell could do.

TWO

I didn't realize how much time I had spent coming up with the rough draft of that spell that morning. In my defense, I never went outside to get to the teashop anymore, or I might've seen how high the sun was in the sky. Since Steph had put a secret door connecting the first floor of the bookshop with the back closet of the teashop, that was my usual route to get to Audrey now.

Houdini might have noticed from where he was napping on the window seat, but when I got up from the table to run down the stairs, he had just leaped up to follow me. The only sound he made was the click of his dog nails on the hardwood floors of the bookshop.

So when I burst out of the teashop closet, waving the parchment covered with the scrawls of ink that were still drying in places, my first impression was that my shout of "Audrey" echoed awfully loudly.

Then I emerged from the back room and saw the dining room beyond was quite empty. There wasn't a single customer at any of the carefully arranged white cast-iron tables and chairs. Not even Barnardo with his little white kitten, Sia. And Barnardo was always there in the morning. He never missed one of our pre-opening get-togethers.

Although, apparently I had. And by quite a bit to judge from the light pouring in through the windows. The sky was mostly gray, overcast with wisps of clouds that threatened to break apart at any moment, but never quite did.

Then I saw Audrey standing at her tea counter, her electric kettle in her hands. Steam curled up out of its spout, so heavily I knew I had caught her just as she was about to pour it into one of her teapots. The fringes of her straight blonde bangs were hanging wetly, clinging to her forehead.

"Tabitha," she said, looking from me to the kettle in her hands to the pot behind her as if uncertain what to do.

"It looks like this one will be a dine-in after all," Liam said as he straightened up from where he had been poking around inside the bakery case. I saw a white paper bag in his hands, but couldn't tell what he had been filling it with.

"Perhaps a different tea," Audrey said, setting the kettle back on its stand, then taking a fresh teapot down from a shelf. "English breakfast?"

"Yeah," I said, still not sure what was going on.

Then Liam slipped the contents of the paper bag onto a plate and handed it to me. I took it with the hand that wasn't holding the parchment and looked down at the four scones piled up there. Two of them were definitely cheddar and something herby, and the other two smelled faintly of apples but strongly of cinnamon.

I was about to mumble a thanks when I finally got a good look at his face. Liam and Audrey shared a pale complexion and propensity for blushing that made every emotion they were feeling very easy to read from their expressions. Audrey had her back to me now, but Liam's face was telling me an entire story.

My sudden arrival was a welcome relief. But more than the flush of sudden emotion that had come with seeing me standing there before him, there were lines of worry around his eyes that my appearance wasn't easing.

And everything about the strange mood in the teashop clicked into place.

"What time is it?" I asked, trying not to sound sheepish.

"Ten thirty," Houdini said primly from where he was sitting beside my ankle.

Well, that was certainly information he could've given me earlier.

I had worried them. Again. The teapot that stood ready for the addition of boiling water that Audrey had pushed aside at my arrival was too far away for me to smell the contents. But I suspected she had been brewing me one of her special teas. Another attempt at getting me out of the funk that she had rightfully assumed I was still in the throes of.

"I'm so sorry," I said, all in a rush.

Liam just nodded, but from the little glances he threw Audrey's way, I knew she was the one I really needed to apologize to. But she was far more consumed with making a simple pot of tea than the task really required of her.

"I didn't mean to worry you. I was on my way down for breakfast when I stopped in my nook. There were a bunch of books there, and I got... caught up," I finished lamely.

"She was in the zone," Houdini informed them. "I did try to get her attention, but it was like I wasn't even there."

Now I was the one with scarlet cheeks as I looked down at the dog beside me. "You did? I'm sorry. I didn't even hear you."

"Apparently," he said with a mental sniff. Which is weird to experience. It's somehow even more chastising than one that doesn't only exist inside your own head.

But then he relented, trotting across the checkerboard tiles of the teashop floor to avail himself of the water dish that Audrey always kept full of fresh water for him and the other dogs who frequented her establishment. "You should probably tell them what you're working on. Maybe with a little more clarity than you were managing upstairs. I honestly couldn't grasp a bit of what you were saying."

"I must've been thinking out loud," I said. I tried to juggle the plate of scones and the parchment both. I was probably a little too focused on not smearing the ink on what was already a very messy bit of calligraphy on the parchment. The plate of scones nearly tumbled to the floor, but Liam snatched it away from me just in time.

"Thanks," I said.

"Whatever it is, it must be quite interesting. I haven't seen you this excited about something in quite some time."

Technically, he was speaking to me. But we both knew from the way he pitched his voice that he was really talking to Audrey.

Audrey sighed, slumping over her counter as if she were too exhausted to carry on with anything in that moment.

Then her timer beeped, and she straightened up at once to pour out the dark black tea.

She turned to hold it out for me, and I saw the worry lines around her eyes were more prominent even than around Liam's.

"I really am okay," I said, afraid to reach out even so far as to take the mug of tea from her hands.

"You do look better," Audrey said grudgingly.

"I feel better," I said. "So much better. I wrote a spell for you."

"Oh," she said. She gestured towards the parchment as if asking permission, and I hurried to exchange it for the mug of tea.

She had made it twice as strong, and added twice the sugar. Just the way I liked it when I needed a pick me up.

And while I wouldn't have thought in that moment that I needed to be picked anymore up than I already was, I realized at the first sip that I had delayed my morning's caffeine far too long.

And with the second sip, I remembered I hadn't eaten anything yet either.

I tried not to lunge at the plate of scones in Liam's hands. But I completely failed to not make a pig of myself, cramming one of the cheese ones into my mouth in two monster bites.

"This is interesting," Audrey murmured as she read over my scrawled words. She held the parchment in one hand so she could tuck her long, straight blonde hair behind her ear with the other.

"What is it?" Liam asked.

"Structural magic is all I could gather," Houdini said.

"Like the spell that made the extra room in our apartment?" Liam asked.

"The same sort of magic, but a different sort of spell," I said.

"We should try it out," Audrey said.

"What, now?" Liam asked.

"Well, the shop is already closed," she pointed out.

Which made my cheeks flush hotly again. They had closed the shop because of me. Because they felt they had to check in on me. Again.

"We can do it later," I said. "I should probably redraft some of the wording, anyway. I think it's a little awkward."

"Nonsense. It's perfect poetry. Same as always," Audrey said.

Her scolding tone made it hard to know how to take the compliment. So I just nodded, then shrugged, then nodded again.

"But what does it do?" Liam asked.

"It creates a living embodiment of the spirit of a place," Audrey said.

"Like, the spirit of the teashop?" he asked.

"That's what I hope it does," I said. "Like a protector spirit that will watch over the teashop and both of you as well. But I think this first version of the spell will maybe only create a momentary ghost kind of thing."

"Household spirits," Audrey said. "One of the oldest kinds of magic. This could be interesting."

"What does the spirit of a teashop look like?" Liam asked. "Will it look like your grandaunt Agatha?"

"I don't think so?" Audrey said, but turned to me with a puzzled frown.

"I don't know," I admitted in an embarrassingly chipper voice. I was way too upbeat, I knew it. But after weeks of feeling so very low, it was nice to feel upbeat again for a change.

Although I wasn't missing the worried glances Audrey and Liam were trading. There was probably such a thing as *too* upbeat, and I should try to tone it down a little.

"Did you want to try it?" I asked between bites of the second cheese scone.

I watched Audrey scan the parchment, her lips moving ever so slightly as she tried out the sort of proto-Norse language that the spells of the Square responded most strongly to.

"We should check with Steph first," she said at last.

"Why check with Steph?" I asked.

But, very much as if saying his name out loud had summoned him, I heard Steph answering for himself from the back room behind me.

"First of all, if the spells touch on the protective magic of the Square at all, you should absolutely check with me first," he said even as I spun to throw my arms around him in a hug.

I felt like I hadn't seen him in days. But I knew it had been one. Less than one, technically. Not quite twenty-four hours.

But he hugged me back so tightly, I was certain it felt like days to him too.

"It's not quite invoking any of that magic, but I don't think the spell will work if the Square objects. So to speak," Audrey said.

Steph half let me go so he could take the parchment that Audrey was holding out to him. I took the opportunity of his momentary distraction to get a better look at him.

He was actually looking really good. Still dressed in black trousers, boots and tunic, so just as Hamlet-esque as ever. And his tall mass of dark curls was not a bit less unkempt than usual.

But compared to the worry-furrowed faces of Audrey and Liam, he looked well-rested and unbothered.

As if he felt me looking at him so intently, he shot me a little sideways glance with his dark brown eyes. There was just a hint of a question there.

"Second of all?" I asked him.

"What's that?" he asked, even as his eyes went back to scanning the text of my spell.

"You said first of all, all that stuff about the Square," I reminded him. "What was the second of all?"

"Oh," he said. "There was the little matter of the emergency call that I wasn't told was no longer an emergency."

He was grinning, but Audrey was flushing darkly.

"I was in the bookshop the entire time," I told him.

"We didn't know that," Audrey said.

"I was in my nook, buried in books. And Houdini was there the whole time," I said.

"We didn't know that," Audrey said again.

Steph just pulled me closer again and planted a kiss on the top of my head.

I had the strange sensation that he had to flatten down my curls a bit to plant that kiss. Like the October air was already the sort of dry I knew it was going to get in the middle of winter, when every doorknob carried a risk of discharging so much static charge. As did my hair.

I was just telling myself I was being silly when I realized he was looking down at me as if trying to gage whether I had felt the same thing.

I touched my hair. No sparks. And it wasn't crazy frizzy.

Did it feel different? Or was I imagining it?

Or was I just hoping to feel a little something like my old chaos magic was returning?

"Am I manifesting?" I asked him, only half joking.

"We should probably swing by the Tower and check in with the Wizard," Steph said. "Not the least because he got the same emergency call I did."

"Her uncles said she wasn't in her room," Audrey said. She was sounding downright defensive now.

I left Steph's side to pull her into a tight hug. "I'm sorry," I said, with all the sincerity I felt in my heart. "I know that I worried you, and I didn't check in like I should have, and you had every reason to think the worst of what I might be up to. I'm truly sorry."

"But you're feeling better?" she asked.

"I am," I said. "Truly. And do you know why?"

"Why?" she asked.

"Because I wrote a spell for you," I said. "And I know it's going to work beautifully, because we're such a perfect team. I can't wait to try it out with you."

"But first, you have to go see the Wizard," she said with a smile. "That's all right. I have a few things I want to arrange here first. I have some thoughts about the spell. But we can talk about it after you've let the Wizard know you're all right."

"Absolutely," I said.

Houdini didn't wait for an invitation. He just leaped into the air, assuming I would catch him.

Which wasn't hard for me to do. I didn't even have to bend over. For a little dog, he had an amazing vertical jump.

Once I had him in my arms, I moved closer to Steph's side. He wasn't wearing his magical, multicolored cloak that allowed him to teleport all around the world. He didn't need it just to get inside the Tower from another part of the Square.

I missed the feeling of the dark weight of its folds closing in around me.

But, as always when I was that close to Steph, the back of my tongue tingled with the flavor of melting butterscotch, rich and sweet.

And then the teashop around us blinked away.

CHAPTER

THREE

I opened my eyes to find us standing in the middle of the Wizard's study in the heart of the library that was the entire top level of the Tower.

The fire behind us was lit as always, the occasional snap and crackle of the burning logs less a giveaway than the fragrant smell of the applewood itself.

And sitting forward in his battered, old wing-backed chair as if he had been expecting us was the Wizard himself. His gnarled hands were folded together over his lap in a gesture of patient listening.

Steph guided me over to the chair opposite the Wizard's with a gentle hand at my elbow, and I sat down with Houdini still in my arms.

"Safe and sound, just as we knew," the Wizard said to Steph.

There was something teasing in his tone, and I was just starting to suspect that Steph had been more worried by Audrey's apparent alarm than he had been letting on. But when I looked back over my shoulder to where he had been, Steph was gone.

Not *far*, he was still in the room. But something on one of the

Wizard's many overflowing tables of books and artifacts had apparently caught his attention and was holding him engrossed.

With his back to me.

"I didn't mean to worry everyone," I said.

"You woke up with a little extra energy?" he asked.

"I guess so," I said. Or started to.

But if there was one thing the Wizard always expected, it was that those around him should speak with more precision than that.

"No," I said, cutting off my own prior thought. "No, not woke up with. I was still feeling down when Houdini and I went downstairs this morning. We were heading down for breakfast in the teashop with the others, when I ended up in the nook instead."

"The bookshop had something for you?" the Wizard said. The inflection at the end was so slight. Like it was just barely a question.

"Some books about structural magic," I said. "I was just going to scan the titles, but then I got curious and started turning the pages. And then I sat down and was sucked in."

"The other way around, actually," Houdini said. "She was standing there reading book after book for most of the first hour before she sat down."

"I didn't respond to being spoken to, apparently," I said and felt another guilty flush to my cheeks.

The Wizard said nothing. He just studied me with an inscrutable look on his face. He steepled his arthritic fingers, then pressed the tips of his index fingers to his lips as his eyes narrowed, as if focusing more deeply on...

What? Something on my face? Or in the magic around me that only he could see?

But then he just sat up again in his chair, brushing a crumb off one of the arms.

"You weren't under the influence of any spell I can see," he said. "Although the bookshop has been very worried about you for some time. I supposed it's pleased with itself, finally finding something so distracting to catch your attention with."

"Finally?" I asked.

"There have been other stacks of books," Houdini told me.

"Steph brought me some," I said. "I was doing research on accounts of things that might be chaos magic."

I knew I sounded defensive, but I couldn't help it. I didn't like the idea that anyone thought I had let an entire month slide by without doing anything productive.

Even if I basically had.

But now Steph was back in my field of view, and was smiling at me in an indulgent sort of way.

"Yes, you went through every book I brought you, but the bookshop was setting other things out for you that you never looked at at all," he said.

"Seriously?" I asked. Because it felt impossible, that there had been books near me that I hadn't even noticed.

"They weren't about chaos," Houdini told me. "Some were about dragons. Most were about teashop-related things. Recipes and such. But you never looked at any of them. Not even the dragon books."

"I'm sorry, little guy," I said, kissing Houdini on his warm little forehead. Being careful, as I always was, not to bother his ears. They stood out like radar dishes and made him look very much like a bat. But he was sensitive about them and preferred not to have them touched.

"They weren't helpful," he said grudgingly. "Or I would've made you look myself."

"Why *do* I feel better today?" I asked. Although I wasn't sure I wanted to know the answer.

But the Wizard just shrugged. "Maybe a thousand little things, maybe nothing at all. Mostly, I think it was the passage of enough time. Just as I told you it would be."

"My power is returning?" I asked, touching my hair again. It felt as soft and manageable as it always did since I had started using the conditioner that Cressida Cade of the Inanna Salon & Spa had given me months before.

But was there a little hint of a spark to my fingertips?

"With more time," the Wizard said with the kindest of smiles.

"More time," I repeated. My words sounded glum, even to my own ears. I gave myself a little shake, then summoned up a smile. "At least that's more time where I'm safe from my father's nefarious intentions. Right?"

But my smile faded again at the glance that passed between Steph and the Wizard.

"Right?" I said again.

"Probably," Steph said.

"You are always safe here, of course," the Wizard said, gesturing at the Tower around us.

"I know," I said. Although with my magic still almost entirely gone, I didn't like my chances at getting inside the stone structure with no doors or windows. The one with such powerful protections around it that even other wizards had a hard time looking directly at it, let alone getting inside.

"Houdini can always get you here," he said, as if reading my mind.

"Houdini can do more than that these days," Steph said.

"What's this?" I asked, not sure what the sudden smile on my boyfriend's face meant. The Wizard was grinning as well.

"Well," Houdini said, shifting his weight from paw to paw as he perched on my thighs. "There is a thing I've learned how to do. A dragon thing."

"You can fly?" I guessed.

"No," he said, sounding deeply disappointed. As if the idea hadn't even occurred to him, but now that it had, he desperately wanted to figure out how to fly.

"It's a more distinctively dragon thing," Steph said.

I didn't need any more of a hint than that. I picked Houdini up and turned him around to look into his brown dog eyes.

"You can breathe a magic breath?" I asked him. "What kind?"

"Any kind," he said.

"What do you mean, any kind?" I asked.

He squirmed out of my light grasp, then hopped down to trot across the floor to the open space in front of the fireplace. It was the least cluttered area of the Tower's library, but that was far from *un*cluttered.

"Is this safe?" I asked, looking at the Wizard and then at Steph.

"It's fine," Steph said with a laughing gleam to his eyes.

"Show her, Houdini," the Wizard said, making encouraging gestures at the little dog, who stood with paws spread wide on the threadbare rug before the fire.

"Right," Houdini said. Then he sucked in a deep breath, filling his little doggy lungs deeply. He held it for a second or two, then expelled it all out again in a cloud of white frost. The cloud was tiny, no bigger than what those little lungs could possibly hold. But even so, a little flurry of snow condensed out of it and dusted the surface of the rug.

"So you *are* a white dragon," I said, secretly pleased that my first guess as to what sort of dragon he was had been correct.

But Houdini took in another deep breath, then exhaled a cloud of fire. He aimed that one a little higher, so as not to singe the rug. But the danger, like the cloud, would have been small either way.

He made a greenish cloud of noxious gas next, filling the library with the sharp smell of something that was poisonous for sure.

Then there was a yellow cloud that smelled of acid, bringing with it a lot of memories of my academy days and certain accidents in various alchemy labs that I would've preferred to have remained forgotten.

But then he blew out another breath that smelled of a high alpine meadow when the wildflowers were in their fullest bloom. I could feel the invigorating coolness of that air, not just over my skin but like it was blowing through my mind and soul, leaving me refreshed.

What sort of dragon blew breath like that?

Then Houdini started coughing, great racking doggy coughs.

"You did overdo it just a bit," the Wizard admonished him.

"I'm quite all right," Houdini said, but even the voice in the back of my mind sounded a little out of breath.

Steph scooped him up, then returned him to my lap, where he promptly curled up and closed his eyes.

"Two breaths in a day was his previous record," Steph said. "But he wanted to show off for you."

"Why didn't I know about this?" I asked.

Not that I needed anyone to say it out loud. I'm sure it would've been one more thing that floated by me, unnoticed. Like stacks of books or the attention of my friends.

"He's been coming in the evening and at night, but only when Steph is with you," the Wizard said.

I cast back in my memories and realized this was likely true. I would've sworn just a minute before that Houdini had been by my side without fail, day and night. But now that I was really thinking about it, I remembered all the times when I had, if anything, assumed he was giving Steph and me a little privacy.

"He's been a busy little dog," I said. "Or, I guess, dragonet. But what does it mean, that he can do the breath of all kinds of dragon?"

"I'm not sure," the Wizard said. "Perhaps it is a side effect of Agatha's spells. Her magic was often an enigma to me."

"He's been pushing hard because he wants to be able to protect you," Steph said. "He might be pushing a little *too* hard, although I'm not sure even you could convince him to ease up even a little."

"Maybe if I'm better now, he'll worry less," I said as I pet his sleeping head.

But when no one responded, I looked up at the Wizard. "What is it?" I asked.

"Perhaps nothing," he said.

"It's about your father," Steph said. He folded his arms as if the air inside the Tower had gotten suddenly cold despite the fire burning just behind him.

"What about my father?" I asked. "Is he finally giving up on the friendly shopkeeper cosplay?"

"No," Steph said. "His Shop of Wonders is doing the same gangbusters business it's been doing since he opened. And he certainly answers anyone who asks about his prior political career that he considers himself totally and completely retired from public life."

"But?" I prompted.

"There are rumors," he said with a glance at the Wizard.

"Not about your father specifically," the Wizard said. "About the old families of dark mages. Like your father's family, the Wards."

"What are the rumors saying?" I asked.

"There may be something brewing among those families. Some sort of.... Well, gang warfare," Steph said with a shrug.

I frowned. "What does that even mean?"

"We've seen hints of this already, when we were dealing with the Talbot Book Repository," he said.

"The Unveiled Guild," I said, and felt a shiver dance up my spine. The Unveiled Guild were thieves and assassins. They had killed Prospero Talbot in order to gain control of blackmail material that had fallen into his possession. And although we had never been able to prove just who had hired them, we knew it had to have been one of the old families with dark histories and the means and motive to cover up the secrets of those histories.

"They've been more active lately," the Wizard said. "So far, no one is dead and nothing that the authorities know of has been stolen. But then again, the things they are likely to steal are things no one should even legally have, so how would we know?"

"But you know they're active?" I asked.

"We can monitor their communications, to a certain extent," the Wizard said.

"You have spies in the Unveiled Guild?" I asked, horrified. Then that horror quadrupled, and I gaped up at Steph in terror.

"Not me," he rushed to assure me. "I've been here with you. In the Square. No, it's not me."

"The point is," the Wizard said, pulling my attention back to him, "the old families are moving against each other. They are preparing for action."

"What sort of action?" I asked.

"That's just what we don't know," Steph said with a sigh. "But odds are, it's not going to be anything good for anyone else who gets caught up in it."

"And my father?" I asked.

"Has met with no one," the Wizard said. "Not even clandestinely. He hasn't left the Square since he arrived, and no one has come inside to see him after hours."

"The shop is watched," Steph added. "If he's speaking to any of his customers in code, it's a very, very good one."

"And my brother?" I asked.

Steph and the Wizard traded another one of those long, quiet looks.

But that was answer enough. As usual, what was going on with my brother Mercutio was a mystery to absolutely everyone.

I rather suspected even our father, for all his power and lack of compunction against using manipulative magic, didn't know.

FOUR

When Steph brought me back to the teashop, Audrey had still not opened the doors on the Minneapolis side to let in the prosaic customers.

But our friend and upstairs neighbor Barnardo was there, which was far from unusual. Barnardo was older than Audrey and me by a decade or more, but we all met for breakfast nearly every morning. And his local knowledge had come in handy more than once when I had found myself tangled up in solving another murder.

As much as he was a part of the same magic world that was my and Audrey's home, he, like us, tended to favor a prosaic way of dressing. Although in his case this meant dressing like a prosaic accountant in middle-of-the-road office wear. Think khakis and button-ups.

This particular autumn midmorning, Barnardo was dressed for the cooler weather. His rich brown cable knit cardigan had probably been really lovely before it had gotten covered in white cat hair and had so many loops pulled out of the weave. He was finally looking his old self after nearly dying from poison two months before, his face filling out now that his cheeks were no longer hollow and his belly rounding out the front of his sweater.

And of course he was there with his little white kitten, Sia. She had only gotten a little bit bigger in the month that he'd had her. But she'd gotten a lot more murderous, zipping around the teashop like a lightning bolt and shredding whatever random pieces of wadded napkin or fallen twist tie she could find.

Houdini went scampering after her at once, although if he was speaking to the cat at all, they were not words he was sharing with the humans in the room. But, knowing Houdini, he was making sure that Sia stayed out of trouble. Although she just barely tolerated his airs of helicopter parenting.

Barnardo gave me a chastising look, but said nothing before pulling me into a hug that was cut short when Sia started trying to eviscerate my shoelaces.

"Sorry," Barnardo said, bending to untangle my laces from her claws so he could pick her up.

"Are you here to help with the spell?" I asked.

"No, just stopped in for a refill," he said, gesturing vaguely towards where Audrey was mixing up the contents of various unlabeled tea and herb containers behind her counter. The smell she was releasing into the air by the stirring up of those dried contents was distinctly medicinal.

"I'm sorry I missed breakfast this morning," I said to Barnardo.

"That did put a bit of a pallor over the meeting," he said. But then there was a gleam in his eye, one I was quite familiar with. "I had so much to tell you all."

"About what?" Audrey asked as she wrapped the small canister of tea she had prepared for him in a sheet of plain brown wrapping paper.

I caught her eye, and although she carefully schooled her features not to reveal it, I knew she was only asking because she felt like she had to make it up to Barnardo, not properly listening to him that morning because she had been preoccupied by my absence.

While I often found Barnardo's news of the Square useful information to have, Audrey had never been a fan of gossip. She was humoring him now.

But if Barnardo had any suspicions about her motives, he wasn't showing it. He just leaned against the counter and lowered his voice to say, "Cressida Cade has been seeing someone. But not just some*one*. No, she's got two someones on the hook."

"Good for her," I said. "Although how she finds time for dating at all, I can't imagine. The Inanna Salon & Spa was crazy busy when there were three of them running it together. Now that Delilah Dale is dead and Cleopatra Manx is under house arrest, I'm surprised Cressida even has the energy to drag herself up to her apartment after closing for the day."

"She's hired someone," Audrey said, which was news to me.

But not, of course, to Barnardo. "Phoebe Cassio is just an apprentice, and part-time at that. But once she's done with school, she should shape up just fine, I think," he said.

"She's still at a magical academy?" I asked with a frown. Most of those schools required all the students to board there, at least during the school week. But with the load of coursework, there were few students who could manage to get away even on the weekends.

"Not even," Barnardo said with a grin. "She attends a prosaic beauty school."

"That's why Cressida was so intrigued by her," Audrey told me. "Phoebe is as magical as any of us. But she's curious about the prosaic world in a way most of us aren't. I mean, I open my doors to prosaic customers. But I don't go out into their world much if I can help it."

"I guess I've been hiding away too much," I said. "I should make a point of stopping in and saying hi so I can meet her."

"You missed the point of my story, though," Barnardo said with the slightest hint of a pout.

"Right, Cressida's two dates," I said. "I'm guessing you know who they are?"

"And it's salacious," Audrey said. She almost managed to make that not sound like an indictment.

"I know one for sure, but I have suspicions about the other," Barnardo said.

"Who do you know for sure?" I asked, taking the bait.

"Titus Bloom," he said with a wide grin.

"Titus is married," I pointed out.

"Separated," Audrey said.

"Like, officially?" I asked.

"He stopped visiting Nell in prison months ago," Barnardo said. "But he only started the process of divorcing her two weeks ago. Just when he started seeing Cressida."

"Well," I said, but I couldn't get the rest of the words out. I wanted to say it was good for him, moving on.

But I couldn't quite do it. I still had a lot of feelings about the Blooms. And while I had mostly forgiven Titus for his role—and accepted his insistence that he hadn't known what Nell was up to—I still had nightmares about that day in his coffeeshop.

His wife had channeled the power of an entity from the under realms. And she had used that power to try to destroy me. If Audrey hadn't been there, and if she hadn't found the capacity within herself to step up her ceremonial magic game in time to save me, I don't know what would've happened.

I mean, I'd like to think that Steph would've gotten there in time to save me.

But in my heart of hearts, I was pretty sure I would've either died there, or had my mind broken in a way I would never have recovered from.

So, yeah. Not a happy memory. And it was a good thing I wasn't a voracious coffee drinker, because I found it difficult to go back inside that store. It was entirely remodeled now, out of necessity after all the damage from that fight, but it still felt the same.

It felt unsafe, being in that space.

"Who's the other guy?" Audrey asked as Barnardo slipped the

wrapped tea canister into his pocket and started to look around for any sign of Sia.

"That, I don't know for sure," he said. "But I suspect she's seeing a prosaic man. A local one who's been stopping in her salon. I've seen him from afar, but when I tried to ask her about him, she pretended not to hear the question."

"Then how do you know they're dating?" I asked.

Barnardo smiled a sly smile. "I could tell. With how close they were standing together, and the way she beamed up at him as they spoke, I could just tell."

"Maybe she's just smitten," Audrey said.

"No, it was mutual," Barnardo said. Then Sia came bolting out from behind the counter, a rather crusty-looking old marshmallow skittering across the tile in front of her like a soccer ball in the control of a master player.

I didn't want to think about where she had found that. Or how long it had been wherever she had found it.

Barnardo bent over and snatched her up as she shot past him with a swift dexterity I wouldn't have thought he even possessed. I expected the kitten to object, but she just clambered up his arm to perch on his shoulder as if the whole maneuver had been her idea.

She left a few more snagged sweater threads in her wake, but Barnardo didn't seem to mind. He just touched his forehead in a gesture reminiscent of a man tapping the brim of his hat to say goodbye.

And then Audrey and I were alone in her quiet, darkened teashop.

"You wanted to try that spell?" I asked her.

Audrey grinned at me. "Absolutely. I'm ready to go."

At first, I thought she meant mentally. But then she ducked into the back room and emerged with a tray on which she had gathered a sparkling clean glass bowl, a pitcher of water, and a single tea light candle.

"What's all that?" I asked.

"I made a few tweaks," she said as she carried the tray to the table closest to the center of the teashop. "Not to the language of the spell, obviously. I don't have your gift for rhyme and flow. But it occurred to me that when I was studying ritual magic at the academy, we always used physical components to anchor the magic. And you tend to skimp on that end."

"Well," I said, then again found I had no more words. As much as the spells I modified for her started out with a list of physical components—like the spell we used to detect poisons, which was focused around a bottle of some sort, for instance—when I wrote from scratch, I never remembered the physical at all.

"It's all right," she said to me as she filled the bowl from the pitcher. To judge from the condensation forming on the outside of that pitcher, she had just taken it out of the refrigerator in her back room. "This is why we make such a good team."

"Sure," I said as I watched her pour the water until the bowl was half-filled, then set the tea light floating on its surface. "But wouldn't the focus of a teashop be more like tea than ice water?"

"Maybe," she said with a careless shrug as she pulled a book of matches out of her pocket to light the candle. "But I'm thinking this spell could work anywhere inside the Square, provided we don't tweak it too specifically to this place."

"You think someone else is going to want to experiment with this?" I asked skeptically.

"You think they won't?" she asked, sounding genuinely surprised.

"I guess I could picture Violenta Court wanting to embody the spirit of her fashion boutique, maybe," I said grudgingly. Violenta used magic to do everything in her store. But she also had no prosaic customers.

"Let's just see how this goes first," Audrey said, and lit the candle floating in the bowl.

Clearly, it was no prosaic tea light. The minute the flame hissed to life, it filled the entire teashop in a flickering pattern of light and shadow. Like we were inside of an aquarium, everything undulating liquidly all around us.

"Wow," I said.

Audrey just grinned.

Then she took out her wand and lifted it. The candle flame lifted up with her, although she didn't seem aware of it. I could tell by the unfocused look to her eyes that she was already concentrating on the words she was about to speak.

It always gives me a shiver, the deep, sonorous voice she uses when she casts ritual magic. It's hard to remember or even imagine that she had barely passed her courses at the academy. Just the sound of her voice is filled with power.

Then she spoke the words I had written all in a scrawl in that proto-Norse variant the Square's spells had been originally cast in. And she made my hasty poetry sound downright classical.

She repeated the words over and over, her cadence rising and falling, until the liquid, wavering light started to coalesce in the middle of the teashop.

For a split second, we both were looking at the ghostly form of what might have been a stooped old woman but also might have been a cat dressed in a woman's clothes. Either way, she was wearing tiny, round spectacles that reflected the dim light with a blinding intensity that made her hard to look at.

She said, "Oh," as if our presence there was surprising her rather than the other way around.

And then she was gone again in a flash.

"Sorry, I lost the focus," Audrey said, all but collapsing into the nearest cast-iron chair.

"No, I need to tweak that wording," I said, sliding into the chair opposite hers. She was pressing a trembling hand to her forehead. I hoped she just felt overwhelmed by what we'd nearly done and wasn't having any nasty after effects like a migraine or a nosebleed.

Not that she'd tell me if she was. I'd have to bug Liam later if I wanted to be sure she was okay.

"I might be out of practice," she said with an attempt at a smile. "We haven't done anything like this in quite some time."

"We haven't done anything like this ever," I corrected her. "I think the growing a room spell was easier. It was more in keeping with what the Square wants to do. This is a little more... off book. Maybe too much?" I finished delicately.

"No, no," she rushed to assure me. "I haven't been keeping up my daily practice. I'll do better next time."

"Yeah, but I'm still tweaking that fourth line," I said. "The double hard consonants there are too awkward a phrasing. No other words come to mind at the moment, but I'm sure I'll have something we can try tomorrow."

"Sure," she said with another tremulous smile. "We can try again tomorrow."

"Are you going to open for business now?" I asked.

"No, I think I'll go upstairs and grab a nap," she said.

Which was possibly the most worrying thing I'd ever heard her say to me.

But then Houdini was suddenly there beside us, blinking up at us with sleepy eyes, his radar dish ears only half-deployed.

"Naps are good," he said. "But I miss having a bed here in Agatha's office. Tabitha, can we head home now?"

Now I felt even worse than before. Worried as I was about Audrey, I had been so caught up in doing the spell together—and before that, in listening to Barnardo's gossip—that I had quite forgotten how hard Houdini had been pushing his own magic back in the Tower.

"Absolutely," I said, scooping him up into my arms. "Naps all around. That's the plan."

Although, for my part, I felt like I had slept more than enough in the last month.

I was ready to be awake. Finally.

FIVE

Houdini napped straight through until dinner. Then, after slowly munching through barely half of his already tiny bowl of dog kibble, he just sat quietly and waited for me to finish my own dinner of beef and sweet potato stew.

The stew was amazing. Or perhaps it was just that, the same as I was finally feeling awake after weeks of being half catatonic, my taste buds were back with a vengeance. But the beef that had been seared and the sweet potatoes that had been oven-roasted before coming together for hours in Frank's slow cooker both had the perfect umami, a fact that the herby sauce highlighted without attempting to compete with it.

I could've easily eaten a second serving. But the sight of Houdini trying to sit up patiently while clearly fighting sleep with every slow blink of his eyes was too much for me. I made do with grabbing a couple of the crusty rolls Marco had acquired fresh from the bakery down in the Square, and stuffed them in my pockets before carrying Houdini up to my attic room.

I had never seen him so exhausted. But he'd been my constant companion all through my own tough days. If I had to carry him everywhere for an entire month, it would still not come close to making up for it.

I settled him on the foot of my bed, the folds of my afghan around him without quite covering him, as I knew he liked it best. He turned around once just to truly claim the sleep nest as his own, then stuck his snout under the knee of his back leg and fell deeply, profoundly asleep.

I petted him for a few minutes to be sure he was resting comfortably. Then I pulled a knit beanie down over my curls, slipped on a duster-length sweater I had gotten at Violenta Court's boutique— oversized with huge pockets of a knit so dense it felt like wearing a blanket, even better than a fluffy robe in my book—and headed out the French window at the end of my bedroom. I stepped out onto the little balcony that was all my own, barely large enough for the chair waiting for me there. I shut the window behind me as soundlessly as I could, then settled into that chair to enjoy those two rolls.

A large, very orange moon was just rising in the east, one of the super-sized harvest moons that was only a few days short of being properly full. I could hear carousing coming from the pub in the far corner of the Square near the base of the Tower, and belatedly realized that this day had been a Saturday. Occasionally that door opened, bringing with it a surge of laughter, chatting and singing as well as a sudden rectangle of warm firelight that spread across the expanse of grass between it and the edges of the orchard. I could only see those details now because the trees in the orchard were nearly done with the process of dropping all their leaves.

But that wasn't the only light I could see off to my right. As I pulled another bite off the roll in my hands, my gaze turned further to my right, to the windows of the Shop of Wonders. My father's shop. There was no longer a line of people standing outside it from opening to closing time, but he was still doing steady business. That door opened and closed with a chime I could just make out when the sounds from the pub hit a lull.

Perhaps if I stayed up late enough, I could see him leave for the night. I could watch as he locked up his shop door, then headed up to the apartment Cleopatra Manx had acquired for him up on the top floor.

I had still never seen him. Not even in a photograph. But I had heard enough descriptions of him, I was sure I would know him at once. An attractive man with silver hair and a penchant for steampunk coats with lots of rows of buttons.

My twin Mercutio looked just like our mother, Serena. He had her height, her prominent cheekbones, her long dark hair and moon-pale skin. All of that on a very male, very "could be a practicing martial artist" frame.

Basically, he had lucked out in the attractive genes department.

I supposed he must favor our father in some ways, too. I just couldn't recognize it looking at my brother, not knowing what our father really looked like.

Me, on the other hand? I guessed I was all Greene. Like my mother had been a family outlier in the looks department and now Mercutio was one, too. But my brown hair and round face and comparatively short frame were all just like my uncle Marco's. And, according to him, my grandparents had both looked the same way.

I had never met them either. And yet, somehow, it was a comfort to me. It felt... safer, somehow. To look like them, who had been by all reports good people. And not so much like my parents. Or like my twin.

I was just chomping in to the second roll when I heard a rustle to my left. Like a breeze was playing through the autumn-dried leaves of the ivy that grew up the cast-iron railing of my little balcony.

Only there was no breeze.

No, as if my thoughts had somehow summoned him, I saw my brother there beside me. I don't know if he had teleported to that rather inconvenient location or if he had climbed that ivy all the way up from the ground eight levels below, but there was no mistaking him as he swung a leg over the balcony and slipped into a space far too small to fit him.

I flew out of the chair and backed to the far side of the balcony. But as badly as I wanted to flee back into the safety of my bedroom, I really didn't want to wake Houdini up.

Although, if my brother was here to make trouble, Houdini would never forgive me for not waking him.

"Relax," Mercutio said, raising his hands to show me they were empty. "I just want to talk."

"I have a phone, and so do you," I pointed out, keeping my hand where it was, ready to fling that French window back open.

"I wanted to talk to you face to face," he amended. "I would've done it during the day, but that wasn't exactly doable."

"The bookshop won't let you in?" I guessed.

"I've been busy during the day," he said. It was hard to tell by the orange light of the moon, but I thought his cheeks were flushing a little. If I had to bet, I'd say he did try to get into the bookshop. And the bookshop indeed had not let him in.

But I decided not to rub that in. "Busy doing what? Working in your shop?" I asked.

Then I took another bite from the roll in my hand. Not so much because I wanted to look casual or anything. It was just like my hunger was unquenchable, despite the warmth of that stew still in my belly.

"I haven't been in that shop," he said, giving me a weird look. Like he couldn't tell if I was joking with him or not.

"So, where have you been?" I asked.

"Looking for our mother," he said. Then he turned away, looking off toward the left, where the shops down below were mostly already closed for business. He let the dark sheet of his hair fall forward, blocking his face from view. And when he spoke again, his voice was barely more than a murmur. "I know what she did to you. I mean, I heard about it. I can't imagine what it felt like for you."

"Can't you?" I asked sharply. "Isn't it basically what you tried to do to me in my nook before you got yourself banned from the bookshop?"

"I was trying to set your power free, not take it from you," he said. But he still wasn't looking at me.

"Same difference," I said. "Either way, it's someone else deciding what happens with my own power. It was wrong."

"I know. I'm sorry."

Then he tossed his hair back to look at me, and I really wished he hadn't. Because the regret there was so real, so sincere, it was like a stab to my heart.

I closed my eyes and reminded myself that everything my brother had ever told me had been a lie.

But it was really hard to believe it.

"Why are you here, Mercutio?" I asked at last.

"You're still in danger. You know that, right?" he asked.

"Is that what you're doing on my balcony? Showing me how unsafe I am?" I asked.

"What? No," he said. "Sorry. I could've come inside, you know. But I've been waiting to catch you out in the open to talk to you."

"You're not really helping your cause here."

"You're right," he said, turning away again and clenching the railing so tightly I honestly feared he'd bend it. "That sounded stalker-y didn't it?"

"You've been waiting for a month for me to come outside so you could ambush me? What sounds stalker-y about that?" I asked.

He barked out a humorless laugh, then said, "Fair enough. Fair enough."

"I'm guessing this is danger from our father you're warning me about? With absolutely no sense of the irony?" I said.

"Yeah," he said. "But look. I've been trying to find our mother. And it hasn't been easy, but I think I have a good lead. If it pans out, I want you to be ready."

I had just put the last bit of roll in my mouth and struggled to swallow it down my suddenly dry throat.

"Ready for what?" I asked as soon as I could make words again.

Because if he meant revenge, he really didn't know me at all.

But then, I already *knew* that he didn't know me at all.

So what *did* he mean?

"We have to talk, the three of us together. And not on phones," he said with just a hint of a sneer. "We have to talk together, face to face. She owes us some explanations, don't you think?"

"I'm not sure I'm ready to hear them, actually," I said. "I haven't been outside for you to catch me for a reason, you know."

"I know," he said, with the full brunt of that anguished sincerity again. "I know you've been... whatever you've been. But things are happening, and we're running out of time."

"What sorts of things?" I asked.

Because if there was anyone who would know about the secret dealings of the old magical families, it was Mercutio.

But before he could answer, a sudden piercing scream rent the night. It was coming from down below, down in the Square.

I was pretty sure it was coming from the heart of the hedge maze.

But when I lunged to the railing to try to peer down, I realized that as suddenly as he had come, my brother had gone again.

Definitely teleportation, then.

But had he honestly wanted to discuss our mother with me? Or had it all been a ruse?

Had he been keeping me distracted so that whatever had just happened below could happen?

But there was no way for me to even guess the answer to that question. At least, not until I knew just what had happened down in the hedge maze.

It was going to be a long run down staircase after staircase to get to ground level for those of us without teleportation magic.

But before I even started that run, I had to wake Houdini. He definitely wouldn't forgive me for leaving him behind. No matter how much of a hurry I was in to get below.

Only maybe it was too late to hurry. Because that scream had ended and not recurred. And in my experience, a single scream was never a good sign.

Houdini had been awake, standing bolt upright on the bed when I came in through the window. But even so, he needed me to carry him down through my uncles' apartment, out onto their veranda, then down the various cast-iron staircases and along the balconies to more staircases, all the way down to the moon-touched grass below.

But we weren't the only ones making the journey. People were emerging from every door we passed, throwing on jackets or coats as they rushed out into the cold night air. I saw Barnardo with Sia in his arms a little ahead of us, giving Titus Bloom a side eye as they passed into the opening of the hedge maze, almost shoulder to shoulder.

"Your father isn't here," Houdini said in my mind, as if he knew why my head was on a swivel. "I would sense him. Your mother isn't here either."

"Mercutio was here," I told him.

And then I wished I hadn't. I felt his little doggy body tense in shock, then slump in defeat in my arms. And I felt absolutely terrible, making him feel like he had let me down.

"He just wanted to talk," I said to Houdini as we finally passed through the arched opening of the hedge maze. "He made himself scarce when we heard the scream."

"Perhaps that's why he didn't rouse me, then," Houdini said after a moment's thought. "If he had no ill intent. That is why I slept on."

I said nothing. But I was pretty sure it was total exhaustion that had kept Houdini sleeping.

It was strange, navigating the turns of the hedge maze in the dark, surrounded by silent people. But there were so many of us streaming through the maze that even someone who didn't know how to get to the center would have no difficulty following the others to get there.

And yet, as much as we all huddled down inside our outerwear in a way that the chill temperature didn't entirely account for, none of us said a word.

In the months since I had come to the Square, the inhabitants had been through a lot. Starting with the death of Agatha and the attempted murders of Audrey and me. Someone in league with an entity from the under realms had been amongst them all for longer than they knew, but my arrival was what had exposed it for all to see.

Then there was the summer party I had brought to an end when my power had started a conflagration. Then Delilah Dale had been murdered in the alley, and I had lost control of my power again trying to escape her murderer in that same alley.

At least all my adventures trying to acquire the book that might have explained my power had involved deaths far from the Square itself.

Only to have Barnardo nearly die from the same poison that had killed his pet matagot, Miss Snooty Cat. That had happened right in his kitchen on the second floor of the Square.

Then the order mage who had longed for revenge for a past grudge against my father had planted a dead prosaic woman inside the Square in a clumsy attempt to frame him for the murder.

But that had been on the fringes of the highest level of apartments.

This, this scream we had all heard, had come from the heart of everything.

People were shaken up. I could feel it. No one was speaking, but it was like we were all too numb.

Or we were all waiting. Because none of us knew yet what was going on.

Then I reached the heart of the maze, where the stone arch stood that marked the location of the magic portal that could teleport mages throughout the world. Most of us came and went through that portal. All of our mail passed through it.

It was our connection to the greater magical world.

Everyone was gathering around it now in still-silent clumps of handfuls of people.

But not because the portal was active and something was coming through it. There was no sign of the rainbow lights of its magic, not now.

But at the very feet of that tall stone arch lay a man, sprawled face-down on the ground.

And slumped beside him, kneeling but with her face hidden by her hands and hair, was Cressida Cade.

She was still and silent, with not so much as a tremor to her shoulders to speak of weeping. And yet, I knew, behind those hands, tears were falling.

And I was pretty sure it had been her scream we had all heard.

I set Houdini down, then walked closer to where Cressida wept over that body.

"Has anyone called the Authorities?" I asked the group at large.

There were a few murmurs. No one spoke up, but I guessed that the common answer was no.

"I'll do it," Titus said, turning to make his way back out of the maze. Presumably to call from his coffeeshop.

He brushed past Audrey and Liam as he left the center of the maze. Audrey looked nearly as dazed as Houdini, like she wasn't sure if she was awake or still napping. Liam had a hand on her elbow in a gesture of support. But once the two of them had taken in the tableau under the arch, they both rushed forward to my side.

"Do we know who it is?" Audrey asked me.

"No," I said, although I had an idea.

It was a good guess that Barnardo had been right about Cressida's dating life. Or, at least, on the right track.

"Cressida?" Audrey said as she dropped to her knees beside the magical beautician. She slipped an arm around Cressida's shoulders.

But it was as if that gentle touch broke some sort of spell. Cressida sat back on her heels, dropping her hands away from her face.

Her eyes were red, but they were dry.

Cressida sucked in a long, shaky breath. Then she said, "I'm all right. I was just startled, is all. I wasn't expecting to see a body here. I was just going to make a quick trip to London to see my mother. I was almost through the portal when I tripped over him. How did he even get here?"

"Is this..." I started to ask, but couldn't find a delicate way to finish that question. So I changed tacks. "Do you know who this is?"

"Yes, but I don't know how he could be here," Cressida said. "He's prosaic. Wendell Gorman, that's his name. He's running for city council or some such prosaic thing. He keeps coming around to the businesses to talk to us about our concerns as his potential constituents. Or, at least, that's what he said he was doing. How did he get in here?"

"He wasn't a special friend of yours?" I asked. Because I had to.

But Cressida gave me a look like she thought I might be crazy. Like dangerously crazy.

"Special friend? No, I barely know him," she said.

I scanned the crowd for Barnardo, but if he was still in the maze, he was far from the center of the scene.

Then I felt a familiar sensation, of air suddenly displaced, and didn't need to turn around to know that Steph was now standing behind me.

"Tabitha," he said breathlessly, as if relieved to find me there.

"You sensed this?" I asked him.

"No," he said with a bitter twist to his mouth.

"That's getting to be kind of common, isn't it?" Someone in the crowd mumbled. I spun around to pinpoint the source, but no one was making eye contact with me.

"Never mind," Steph said to me in a low voice. "They're not exactly wrong, are they?"

"Another dead prosaic inside the protective spells," I said. "Faerie magic again, do you think?"

"No," he said. Then he sighed tiredly. "Every time something like that happens, the Wizard and I tweak all the protections. Which means every time something like this happens again, it has to be something new. New, but powerful."

"He really is running for city council," Liam said, his face lit brightly by the screen of the phone he was studying. "Wendell Gorman. Local business owner and property developer, looking to take the seat of one of the incumbents. With money to burn in the pursuit, to judge from the quality of his website and PR team."

"Was this some sort of political assassination?" Steph asked.

Liam laughed drily. "Doubtful. This is Minneapolis, not Gotham. How did he die, though?"

We all looked down at the body, still lying face-down on the dry autumn grass.

There was no sign of any injury. But from the arrangement of his legs right next to each other and his arms straight at his sides, I didn't think he'd fallen here.

No, someone had placed him here. In fact, it looked like he had been rolled up into a carpet and put here, and then the carpet had been disappeared. His posture was just so tucked in tight.

"Volumnia is on her way," Houdini told us. Volumnia was the old weird woman who took care of the dead in our neighborhood. From the way his nose was up in the air, it was like Houdini smelled her coming. But I saw no sign yet of the eerie green glow of her chained lantern. She had to be at least a couple of turns away inside the maze.

"Titus went to call the sheriff already," I told Steph.

He nodded even as he studied the body before us.

"This is going to be like before, isn't it?" I asked. "Like with the prosaic murder victim a month ago, Gia Bryant? This Gorman guy is just going to end up dumped in the alley for the prosaic authorities to deal with?"

"Only if we determine first none of us magical types were involved," Steph said. "And only after our authorities have communicated through the back channels with their authorities. It's really more of a hand-off than a dumping, or as much like that as we can make it and maintain the necessary secrecy of our home."

"I know," I said. And now I was the one heaving a tired sigh. "I know. I just wish there was a better way."

Or that our magical authorities weren't so chronically overworked that investigating a dead prosaic stood some chance of being a priority.

But I already knew it wouldn't be. Unless Volumnia quickly turned up signs that this man had been killed by magic, he was going to end up shunted into the alley.

And the prosaic police wouldn't be able to come inside the Square. Which, I had a feeling, was going to be pretty important in solving the crime.

Welcome to the niche in the world that I had somehow found myself filling.

It was a good thing I was still riding the wave of my newfound alertness. I had the feeling I was going to need all my faculties in the next few days.

Volumnia ghosted her way into the heart of the maze then, seeming to glide over the grass, the lantern hanging from its chain in her hand not so much as swaying with her motion. As always, she appeared to be in her whitest nightgown, her long silver hair hanging loose all around her.

Her face looking older than time itself. She was always an unnerving presence. And not just because I only ever saw her when there was a body to be examined.

And cared for, I reminded myself. Caring for what the dead left behind was her real mission. Even the ones like this prosaic man who weren't destined to be interred in her catacombs under the Square.

She was still silently examining the body without touching it when Sheriff Jane MacMorris arrived, Deputy Eric Fluellen in tow.

Then the crowd finally dispersed, but only because MacMorris, in her booming voice, told us all to go back to our beds.

And I didn't miss the pointed look she threw my way. Apparently, that order went double for me.

Which was fine with me. Examining the body wasn't anything I could help with. And the bureaucracy of starting an investigation was definitely not my area of expertise.

But when all of that wound down, if nothing had been learned to bring a killer to justice?

That was where I would step in.

And I knew I'd be starting with a conversation with a certain Titus Bloom.

CHAPTER
SEVEN

To my immense relief, Houdini was feeling better in the morning. We were both up before dawn, full of energy, if for different reasons.

"Barnardo knew things about this man he didn't tell us, don't you think?" Houdini asked me while chowing down his breakfast at record speed.

It was a neat trick he could do, talking in my head even while his doggy mouth was busy eating. The rest of us were compelled to finish chewing before we could speak.

"If he didn't yesterday, I guarantee he knows more now," I said. I was drinking instant coffee just for the caffeine hit, leaving the rest of my breakfast for when we went down to the teashop.

But that was still an hour away. I'd definitely be hitting my nook first. And if the bookshop had left out more books for me, I'd be glad I had that little bit of caffeine first.

"It must have been someone who lives in the Square who brought that body inside this time," Houdini said with the air of great authority. "The Wizard has told me so much about how he maintains the spells around the Square, and I just don't see how else it could have gotten there. Even if it were a magical person, if they didn't live here, the Square would've raised an alarm. I just know it would have."

I said nothing. I *wanted* to agree. I knew how powerful the Wizard and Steph both were. And I definitely knew how hard they both worked to maintain the safety of the Square for all of us.

But I was starting to learn other things too. Like how powerful evil people could also be. And how hard they worked to do what they did. To do it, and get away with it both.

It almost didn't seem fair. They could keep trying and trying, and the spells that maintained the Square could keep shutting them down and shutting them down.

But they only had to succeed once. And then everyone was blaming the Wizard and Steph.

I mean, faerie magic is so incredibly rare. And yet Lucentio Stanley had used an artifact he had stolen from faeries to get the dead body of Gia Bryant inside the Square.

Of course, he had paid a price for that. The faeries have no forgiveness in their hearts for theft of any kind. Whether he would've been processed by magical or prosaic authorities was a question that became moot when the faeries came for him themselves.

So what was it this time? What could be rarer than faerie magic?

And what price would such magic come with?

I actually shivered just at that thought. Then I drained the last of my coffee, let Houdini leap up into my arms, and headed down to my nook.

There were no new books there, but all the books I had used the day before to craft the spell for Audrey were still waiting for me, sprawled open to all the most relevant pages just as I had left them.

At the same instant that I remembered I wanted to tweak that spell, I realized just how I wanted to do it.

But knowing how it should be done and actually doing it weren't exactly the same thing. I had to sit down with some of the denser tomes of proto-Norse spellwork to craft it all.

I didn't go down the same rabbit hole this time, though. I tweaked the line that had bothered me the most when I had heard Audrey speak it out loud, then polished a few of the other lines as I rewrote the whole thing on fresh parchment, making my best effort to keep my writing neater this time.

When I was done, I set my pen aside and held up the parchment to look it over one last time as the ink dried. I spoke aloud the words I had written, just to hear the rhythm and the rhyme aloud.

But I felt something, speaking those words. Not that I was actually casting the spell, nothing remotely as powerful as that.

No, it was just a little stirring, deep in my soul. But it wasn't a stirring that was responding to the poetry.

It was responding to the magic.

The feeling was gone as quickly and mysteriously as it had come. But it had been there. I had felt it.

I wasn't going crazy.

My mother hadn't taken everything from me. And now what little I had been left with was starting to grow again.

I looked back at the books I had left neglected at the other end of my study table. All the books with references to magic that just might be chaos magic. I had half-filled a journal of my own with all my notes. But I was going to have to get back to it, and soon.

My power was coming back. It would take some time to properly arrive, but I swore I would be ready.

This time, I would be in control of all of it. Somehow.

Houdini had been napping in his chair at the head of the table, but at five minutes to seven, he poked his nose over the edge of the table to look at me.

"I'm ready," I told him before he even said a word. "See, I'm not ignoring you at all today."

"Yes, I appreciate that," he said with just a glimmer of humor in his tone.

I rolled up the parchment and tucked it in my back pocket, then picked Houdini up again to carry him down to the first floor and through the secret door to the back of the teashop.

I heard Barnardo's voice before I was even out of the closet in the back room, his tone excited and eager, even as his words were too muffled for me to quite catch them.

I was momentarily confused when I saw Audrey and Liam both in the back room, Liam pulling one set of pans of scones out of the oven while Audrey waited to replace them with a second batch.

Who was Barnardo talking to out in the dining room?

For one horrifying moment, I thought Mercutio was back.

But I was only willing to hear him out because he was, despite everything, still my brother. Barnardo had no such ties. And, frankly, was not the most forgiving person I'd ever met.

Not that he blamed Mercutio for the poisoning that had nearly killed him. But he tended to lump all the old families together in one evil category, be they Ward like my brother, or Manx like Cleopatra, the woman who had actually put the poison in his cream.

Still, I was so consumed with the idea that I needed to get out there and drive my brother away from my friends that I charged past Audrey and Liam without so much as a good morning.

And nearly collided with Steph, who had been looking back over his shoulder at the still chatting Barnardo even as he attempted to get behind the counter.

I suspected he had been planning to offer to help in the back, if only to escape Barnardo.

But finding me suddenly in his arms was clearly the better diversion.

"Hello," he said. Then looked down at Houdini, still in my arms between us. "Two breaths a day, max, little guy. And nothing today. Agreed?"

"I make no promises," Houdini said pompously. "I have no idea what this day will require."

"Perhaps less showing off, then?" Steph suggested.

Houdini made a sputtering sound, like a tickle in my brain.

Clearly, the idea that he had been showing off the day before didn't sit well with him at all.

And yet, he couldn't quite deny that had been exactly what he had been doing.

"No promises," was all he got out in the end. Then he shifted his weight around enough to give me the hint that he wanted to be on his own paws.

I set him down, and he immediately trotted over to where Sia was batting at the surface of the water bowl with one claws-extended paw. What her kitty-cat brain thought she was doing was a mystery, but she was very intent at it.

"News?" I said to Steph as he reluctantly let me steer him back to our table, where Barnardo was just pouring out the tea Audrey had brewed for us all. Something lemony from the smell, but also strong because that was what Audrey always brewed in the morning.

"He wouldn't tell me anything," Barnardo said petulantly. "And it's not like we don't know he's got something to say. He's here, after all."

"I come to breakfast as often as I can be spared," Steph said.

"We know," Audrey said as she came in with two plates of fresh scones in her hands. "It's just, it's a little suspicious that today you can be spared. Given all that happened yesterday. Feels like you'd be busy."

She gave him a teasing smile that did nothing to ease the squirming discomfort I just knew he was feeling.

"She's not wrong," I said as we sat down at the table. "Spill."

"Wendell Gorman is still in Volumnia's preparation chamber," he said. "There is absolutely no sign as to what killed him. It's as if his heart just stopped beating. Only, for a man of his age, his heart was in remarkably good shape."

"So, magic?" Liam guessed.

"No, she would sense that," I said. "What does it mean that she can't?"

"She's still looking into it," Steph said. "But Sheriff MacMorris has given her until this afternoon to either find something or give up. The longer we do nothing, the harder it is for the prosaic authorities to take up the case later. It's a balancing act."

"Do we even know where he died?" I asked. "Because I just don't think it was right there, in front of the portal. People move through there all the time, day and night. Unless this was a spontaneous thing, no one planning a murder would choose a place so unlikely to guarantee privacy."

"It might have been spontaneous," Barnardo said with a mischievous gleam to his eye. "A crime of passion."

"You can't be thinking of Titus," I said. "He was outside the maze with the rest of us. He, in fact, entered the maze at the same time you did."

"Or so he would have us think," Barnardo said. "He could've run outside, then blended in with the crowd coming in."

"Steph, what about the spells that hold the Square together?" Audrey asked. "Is everything okay there?"

Steph didn't answer for a painfully long time. Then he took a long drink from his teacup before finally saying, "Nothing appears to have been disrupted."

"But the Square built all those escape routes," Audrey said. "I can't stop thinking about that. I mean, one of the most prominent ones comes out of my apartment. Maybe because it still thinks of it as Agatha's apartment? Or it's worried about me in particular?"

"The Square isn't a sentient being with feelings like that," Steph said. "We humans might think we perceive something going on there, but we're just projecting."

"It created escape routes," I said. "You said so. It did that."

"Yes," he said. I could tell he had the squirming discomfort feeling again, but I didn't relent. "It's hard to explain," he said almost desperately. "But thinking of it as something you can talk to, to ask questions and get answers, that's not going to be helpful."

"My bracelet," I said, then broke off. I wanted to say that a scone crumb had caught in my throat, but I knew that wasn't true.

I missed that bracelet so much. It had kept me safe. It had helped me control my power. And it had deserved better than getting ground to bits under my mother's heel.

"My bracelet communicated with me," I said when I was sure my voice wouldn't waver again. "Not in words. And I guess you're right, it wasn't exactly in feelings either. But it was something. And we understood each other."

"In a limited way, yes," Steph said. "I know the Wizard understands the Square better than I do, but honestly, I don't know how less limited it is than your bond with your bracelet. I suspect it might be more limited. Because the Square's made up of so many, many more spells than what were in the links of your bracelet."

"I don't think this is the event," Liam said after we'd all been silent for too long. "It's tragic, and I do hope we figure out what happened to Wendell Gorman and find justice for him. But this can't be what the Square was worried about."

And then we were all silent again, lost in our own thoughts.

Because none of us disagreed with him at all. But just what the Square was preparing for was impossible to imagine.

And it was too scary to even try.

CHAPTER

EIGHT

As usual, Steph was summoned away from our breakfast gathering before he'd finished a single cup of tea. Audrey wrapped a good half-dozen scones in one of her cloth napkins and forced him to put them in his pocket for later before she'd let him leave. He took them, disappearing the whole thing inside a pocket far too small to contain that many baked goods.

Then, with one last quick kiss for me, he was gone.

"I hope he can figure out what's going on with the Square," Audrey said with a sigh. "It's been a low-level worry for me for the last month, but I think now it's ramping up to a more 'keeping me up at night' kind of level."

"It'll be all right," Liam said, giving her hand a squeeze before getting up to start clearing the table.

"What do you think?" I asked Audrey in a tone that really meant, "What do you want to do now?"

I could tell by the way that her eyes quickly darted over to Barnardo and then away again that she had caught my meaning entirely.

Just like I had caught hers.

55

We both wanted to go talk to Titus Bloom. But we didn't want Barnardo tagging along.

I mean, we both loved Barnardo dearly. And his information, as much tainted as any bit of gossip by its relative truthfulness being unreliable and hard to define, was still of value in finding places to dig for the solution to a mystery.

But he had no ability to set his own preconceived notions aside, and he couldn't hide his feelings. At all.

Trying to talk to Titus with Barnardo there, projecting his already confirmed judgment in Titus's guilt, would be less than useless.

And yet, neither of us just wanted to tell him so.

"Sia looks like she's ready for a nap," Audrey said.

The white kitten in question was coming out from behind the counter at a slow trot. But not really of her own volition. Houdini was behind her, following closely with the watchful gaze of a sheep-herding dog. He wasn't touching her now, but she clearly had been pushed a little to get her moving.

Or, at least, so I judged from the upward lift of her nose. She was a picture of a cat taking great offense.

"She does look worn out," Barnardo said with a cluck of his tongue, getting up from his chair to scoop up the little cat and cuddle her close in his arms.

"Nothing that a spot of warm milk and a long morning nap won't sort out," Houdini said sagely.

"Do you think she's coming down with something?" Barnardo asked, turning Sia in his arms so he could look into her eyes.

Sia flinched ever so slightly, as if a sudden pang of headache had struck her. But then she looked up at Barnardo with her biggest, most imploring kitty-cat eyes.

"Right, I'm taking her upstairs. Right now," Barnardo said.

"Let me know if you need me to try brewing anything for her," Audrey said as she rushed to open the door for Barnardo. "Cats don't really care for tea, but Agatha has a few emergency remedies we can try. But I'm sure Houdini is correct. She'll probably be just fine after a little rest."

But Barnardo was too out of sorts to even muster up an answer. He just pulled the folds of his cardigan around the trembling form of Sia in his arms and hustled through the cool autumn morning, across the Square to the staircase that led up to his second-floor apartment.

"Houdini?" I said the moment Barnardo and Sia were out of sight. "I thought you couldn't communicate with Sia. And yet it looked like you just did something there."

"I can talk to her just like I can talk to you," Houdini said. "She just understands that the same as any cat understands things you say out loud."

"So you didn't just convince her to play sick to get Barnardo out of our hair?" Audrey asked, not quite smiling.

"Well," Houdini said. "Whatever I did, your goal was achieved."

"Thank you," I said, even as Audrey fetched one of her baked dog treats from behind the counter and put it on a plate so he could eat it at the table.

From the smell, I was pretty sure it was peanut butter and bacon. His favorite flavor.

But Barnardo wasn't the only problem that I could see.

"Audrey, you never opened your shop yesterday. Are you really going to stay closed for two days in a row?" I asked.

"I'll open late," she said with a shrug that was not as carefree as I'm sure she intended it to be. "How long could talking to Titus take?"

"You don't even need to do that," Liam said as he came back from carrying our breakfast dishes into the back room to fetch the now-empty plate in front of Houdini. "I don't work until this afternoon. I can open the shop for you and watch things until then. No special blends for your magical customers, obviously. But I can keep your prosaic business going."

"That would be lovely. Thank you," Audrey said, kissing him on the cheek. Which, despite the fact that they'd been living together for a month now, still made him blush in a way I couldn't help but find endearing.

"I can even do a little more online research after the rush," he said. "My laptop is in the office."

"Perfect. Because I don't think we know nearly enough about Wendell Gorman," I said.

Audrey fussed over a few more details in her teashop, Liam taking her instructions good-naturedly even when she gave him the same ones more than once.

And then we were finally off, Houdini trotting along close by my ankle. He kept a constant sweeping surveillance all around us, even though Audrey and I had, without exchanging a word between us, both elected to walk past the bookshop to get to the coffeeshop rather than cutting through the center of the Square.

Because that path would bring us closer to the Shop of Wonders than either of us wanted to be. Even with half of the orchard for cover, that route felt too exposed.

The bookshop wasn't much to look at on the Square side. It was just seven stories of brick and stone, with no windows or decorative features. Even the door to get inside was understated, looking more like an employees-only sort of side entrance than like the customer's main entryway.

Beyond the bookshop was the Inanna Salon & Spa. It sat on the corner of the Square, which being next to the wide expanse of the bookshop and behind the tall hedges of the maze, felt tucked away and quiet. But on the prosaic side of things, it dominated the corner of two major streets. It was no wonder they did such a brisk prosaic business. And I could totally understand why Cressida had made the decision to hire a prosaic-friendly witch to be her apprentice now that she was alone in that shop.

Despite the early hour, there were already customers in all three of the salon's chairs. Unlike Cleopatra, who had ruled her domain from behind the tall counter at the back of the shop, Cressida was right there in it. I could see her long blonde hair swishing this way and that as she spun from one customer to the other, somehow clipping away at what looked to my untrained eyes like a pretty complicated layer cut while also supervising her employee as she sectioned and foiled another customer's hair in the middle chair.

At least the customer in the third chair was in a setting phase, scrolling through her phone with her hair poking out of its own layers of foil in crazy clumps.

"That must be Phoebe Cassio," I said to Audrey as we walked past the glass doors, tipping my head towards the young witch with the short, spiky red hair who was folding a square of foil over a lock of her customer's hair with her tongue just poking out from between her teeth in concentration. "I know this sounds weird to say since we just graduated ourselves, but doesn't she look young?"

"Well, we were in magical academies for four years longer than she was," Audrey pointed out. "Not to mention she's technically not finished. She's going to that prosaic school. So she looks young because she is young."

"I suppose," I said. "I guess I thought she'd be older, given how much responsibility Cressida is putting on her shoulders."

"She must be capable of handling it," Audrey said with a shrug. "Cressida spent a long time reviewing her applicants. Or so I've heard."

"From Barnardo," I said.

"Right," Audrey said, and we shared a smile.

But we were already standing outside the Bitter Brew Coffeeshop, and that smile faded pretty quickly.

I had been back inside that shop only one time since the battle where I had nearly been crushed by the magic of an entity from the under realms. Nothing had happened that second visit. Titus had explained to me how the magical transportation system in Minneapolis worked, and directed me to the station under the pub where I could get on one of the pilot-less boats that navigated the sewers and underground streams of the Twin Cities. He'd even given me a free cup of coffee before sending me on my way.

The entire encounter had been one of helpful kindness. Nothing terrible had happened.

But as Audrey and I stepped inside the coffeeshop that October morning, that visit was not the one I was remembering.

No, it was the earlier one. The visit that had started much like this one was about to, with just a few questions, but had ended in a battle just to keep breathing.

I especially remembered the moment I had watched Titus Bloom's mild-mannered wife Nell morph into something inky dark, sleek but immense, formless in the way so many deep-sea creatures tend to be.

Her inky magic had filled the air of the shop, making it feel close to the point of claustrophobic. And the pressure had just kept building and building.

"I'm here," Houdini said, touching his nose to my ankle.

And just like that, the spell of that memory was broken. Because that terrible moment had been terrible in part specifically because Houdini hadn't been there. He had been trapped outside, unable to get to me.

But he was with me now.

And more than that, both he and I were so much more now than we had been then.

I had thought then that I was a witch without magic, a witch with little power and absolutely no control.

And Houdini might have suspected he was more than the dog he appeared to be, but none of us had yet discovered that he was a dragon hidden in dog form.

I looked down at him to give him a grateful smile, and he puffed out the white star of his chest as if to remind me he could breathe dragon magic now if he needed to.

And I felt better. Although I was still hoping this would be more like my second visit than that other one.

There was a short line of prosaics waiting in sleepy silence for their turn at the counter. Titus Bloom had no employees. Every beverage was one he created then handed over the counter with his own hands.

And if any of the sleepy prosaics noticed he was producing these beverages with atypical speed and finesse, none of them so much as raised an eyebrow.

In part, I supposed they were just his regulars. They'd seen it all before.

But mostly, I was sure there was magic in the whole shop that just kept them from noticing. It was the sort of spell the Square would absolutely help reinforce for him. Anything to keep all of us magic types from being noticed.

Audrey and I waited at the back of the line as if we, too, were there for coffee. And as we waited, I took in all the details of the space around us.

It was possible that his wife had brought an oppressive atmosphere with her wherever she went even when she wasn't actively channeling the under realm entity's power, or perhaps Titus had made more changes in the remodel after the fight than I was picking out with my inexpert eyes. But the whole place just felt more inviting than I remembered it.

I mean, the customers in there now were clearly the early morning crowd, here to grab something in a to-go cup and rush off to work or school or whatever. But with all the nooks of cozy sofas and chairs, the scattering of well-loved paperbacks on side tables and little shelves, and the warm glow of the lamps that were just perfect for reading or for games spread out on the square tables, it felt like a great place to while away an afternoon or evening, alone with a book or together with some close friends.

Titus himself looked just as I remembered him, anyway. Tall and olive-skinned, about a decade older than Barnardo, but trim if not exactly athletic. His hair was still perfectly jet black, as much of it as he still had on the back and sides of his head. Not a single strand covered the top of his head, although I had to give him points for not trying to comb any of those thick, dark locks over that sizable bald patch. The temptation must be great.

After serving the young woman in front of us, sending her off with a steaming beverage that filled the air with the unmistakable aroma of pumpkin spice, he finally turned his attention to us.

I watched his warm brown eyes lose a little of their sparkle as he realized without saying a word that we weren't there to order any coffee.

He glanced past us. Not rudely, just to check if there was anyone waiting behind us to be served.

There was not.

"Right," he said with a little nod.

And somehow I knew just what he meant. Of course, there were no customers behind us. Because we had things to ask him, things the Square also wanted answered.

And, whether through artfully hiding the door from the notice of the prosaics, or some other more aggressive magic, it had made sure that Titus was free to answer those questions.

But also, no more customers would be coming until he did so.

It felt kind of nice, having the entire Square as backup.

I just hoped we weren't going to need more than a little prosaic-redirecting magic. I just hoped this interview wasn't going to end like the last one.

But, glancing over at Audrey and then down at Houdini, I knew we were all prepared. Just in case it did.

CHAPTER

NINE

Titus turned his back to us for a moment, but with no prosaics left inside his coffeeshop, he had no need to hide what he was doing. His hands danced through the air, not quite touching anything but guiding the process as two mugs filled themselves with hot espresso, steamed milk, and all the syrups and flavorings to make two servings of pumpkin spice latte.

I'm not usually a coffee person. But when he set those steaming mugs on the counter and that aroma washed over me, I admitted that usually bitter beverage definitely had its moments.

"This is about Wendell Gorman," he guessed, then took a sip from a mug of his own. From the sight and smell of it, I guessed it was straight black coffee, a dark French roast.

"Yes," I said, wiping a bit of milk foam from my mouth.

"We know he was a prosaic man running for some sort of local government," Audrey said.

"City council," I put in.

"So we thought he might have stopped in to see you at some point," Audrey said.

"And maybe you could tell us something about him," I concluded.

We traded the slightest of nods with each other, then both of us took another sip of those perfectly spiced lattes.

"He's been in all the shops," Titus said.

"Not mine," Audrey said.

"I don't think he was in the bookshop either," I said. Although I didn't know that for an absolute fact. But if he had, I felt like one or the other of my uncles would've mentioned it to me.

"Maybe just up and down our street, then. Perhaps only the shops on this side would be in his jurisdiction? I'm not sure exactly how these prosaic things work," Titus said.

"Any idea how he ended up inside the Square?" I asked as casually as I could.

"Not just inside the Square, but in the very heart of the maze. Right at the portal. The very last place we'd ever want a prosaic to wind up for any reason," Titus said. "No. I have no idea. It's, frankly, quite upsetting."

"The Wizard and Steph are working on it," I assured him.

"I know," he said. Then he sighed heavily. "It's just... This has been such a year for unprecedented things. The accumulation of it all is growing exhausting."

"Did this Wendell Gorman seem like he knew anything about the Square?" I asked. "I mean, the protection spells that keep prosaics from noticing things are very strong. But sometimes there are borderline prosaics who are more sensitive than others. They see things they aren't supposed to. Do you think he might have been one of those?"

"No," Titus said, without even taking a moment to think about it first. "No, he was the most perfectly mundane prosaic I can ever recall encountering."

"What do you mean?" Audrey asked with wide, curious eyes. And I was glad she had spoken first, because I had heard an edge to his voice that I had been about to directly confront him about. But her more oblique way was the better call.

I tried to match her innocent questioning look as I waited for him to answer.

He flushed a little at our unwavering attention. He even pulled at the collar of the button-up shirt he wore under his gray cashmere sweater, as if it had suddenly grown too tight.

But then he just shrugged. "Perhaps it's because he was a politician. He struck me as someone who spoke more than he listened. He definitely projected to be seen more than he saw. All surface, no substance."

"I heard he was attractive," Audrey said, which was a surprise to me. Until I realized she was just guessing.

Titus's deepening flush told us both she had hit the mark, though.

"Some might consider him attractive," he said. "On a surface level. I suppose."

"So if he was working his way up and down this street, he must've stopped in at LeBeau's Bakery and the Abergavennies' Cornershop," I said. I took a quick sip of latte before adding, "And I suppose he chatted with Cressida next door in the salon too."

That earned me another dark flush to Titus' cheeks.

"Perhaps more in one place than another," was all he said.

But, really, that was answer enough.

"You've been seeing Cressida?" Audrey put in.

Titus scowled. "The only person who would've told you that is Barnardo Daley," he said. "No princess was half as capable of spinning straw into gold as that man is of spinning fictions out of the smallest of happenings."

"He does love to gossip," I said. "What nugget of truth is there to his story this time?"

"I've met with Cressida, in public," he said. "But only to discuss our respective businesses. We are not, nor have we ever been, dating."

"It did seem odd to us," Audrey said. "Cressida is so busy since Delilah died and Cleopatra is under house arrest. How could Cressida have time for a new relationship?"

"Oh, I'm sure she could find a way if she were sufficiently motivated," he said.

But that edge was back in his voice.

Oh, how I longed to ask him if there were feelings, but only on one side. I just couldn't figure out a way to phrase it that wasn't going to make him angrier and less likely to answer our questions than the other way around.

I looked at Audrey, the more diplomatic member of our little duo. But she just gave me the smallest of shrugs. She was stymied too.

"Where did Barnardo see the two of you meeting, then?" I asked. "I mean, for him to jump to such a big misunderstanding, did it *look* like you were on a date?"

"We were here, inside my own shop. Because it made more sense to meet to talk where there was coffee rather than where there was..." he trailed off, a single hand dancing through the air vaguely.

Vaguely, but in a way that somehow made it clear that he found the smell of all the beauty products inside of the salon a bit overwhelming.

Or maybe I was just projecting. Because when I went in there, I found it overwhelming myself.

"You met here... twice?" Audrey guessed.

"That sounds right," Titus said with a nod. "Right over there, at that table by the window, if it matters to you."

I glanced over my shoulder at the table in question, but there was nothing unique about it. It was just one of a row of two-tops with two tall stools drawn up to it. Unlike the cozy nooks, it was more a place for someone who didn't want to drink on the go, but had no intention of lingering inside the shop for long either.

Although, given that the glass in question looked in on the Square, I wondered what a prosaic would perceive if they sat there.

Or if they'd even remember later anything they'd seen at all. Maybe a vague memory of a tall, featureless hedge.

But I pushed those musings aside and refocused on what had brought Audrey and me here in the first place.

"Wendell Gorman," I said. "When he came in here to speak with you, what did he have to say?"

"A lot, and yet nothing," Titus said. "He said he came to listen. That he wanted to hear what the challenges were for local business owners. At first, I wasn't sure how to answer. I can certainly pretend to be only concerned with the prosaic side of my business for a moment or two, but how long could I bother trying to sustain that? But in the end, it didn't really matter."

"Because of what you said before," I guessed. "He was more of a talker than a listener."

"Exactly," Titus said, with a bitter twist to his mouth. "I would half get a sentence out, but then he would jump in, guessing where I was going and presenting me with his own solution before I could even finish expressing my thought."

"Was he a good guesser?" I asked.

Titus barked out a laugh, then grew sober once more. "No. Although perhaps other prosaics find him more personable. I can't account for everyone's taste."

And there was that hint of an edge to his voice again.

"Were you there when he called on any of the other Square businesses?" Audrey asked.

"No, he came down during business hours, so I was in my own shop running my own business the entire time," he said.

I glanced back at that two-top table again, then wandered over there to get a better sense of the view.

"You and Cressida sat here because she was keeping an eye on the salon," I guessed. Because from where I was now standing, I could just get an angle inside the salon.

"Yes," he said. "And yes. I saw her speaking with him when he called on her. But I can't tell you a single thing they said."

"No, but you probably got a good read on the body language," I said, still peering through the windows. I could make out Cressida now, chatting with Phoebe as they worked. I could see how she smiled, then laughed at something Phoebe said.

"I don't know. I suppose so," he said crossly.

"Barnardo has seen them together as well," Audrey said. "He said they had a vibe. Mutual attraction, maybe?"

I spun back around before Titus could answer to add, "Or maybe Barnardo was misreading things again? Maybe Cressida didn't catch what you did about what kind of man this Wendell Gorman was."

"Cressida is no fool," he said. How did he manage to make those four words sound both irritated and fond at the same time?

"Even the best of us can get taken in by someone with powerful charisma, if just for a little while," Audrey said.

Titus sucked his teeth loudly but said nothing.

"We should really talk with Cressida," Audrey said to me in a stage whisper.

"That does make sense," I agreed, turning to look at the woman in question through the double layers of windows again.

"I'm sure she had nothing to do with any of this," Titus said. "Whatever 'this' is. Do we even know for sure it was a murder?"

"We only know he's dead, and he was found where he shouldn't be, inside the Square," I said. Not adding that we knew a bit about the timing of those events. I was curious what he would say.

"Look, I understand you're here because you want to rule me out as a suspect. We've been here before, haven't we?" he said, but without any hint of anger. "And, living alone now as I do, I can't offer you any kind of alibi. I don't know how I'd prove that I didn't lure that prosaic inside the Square to kill him at the portal. I can only tell you again that I had absolutely no reason to."

"Not even to protect Cressida?" Audrey asked.

"Cressida isn't in any danger," he said. "Do you have any idea how much power that woman has? I think she could give even Cleopatra Manx a run for her money. Don't be fooled with the frippery she channels most of her magic into. She can do far more than that if she's compelled to. No, Cressida was never in any danger. Certainly not from a prosaic."

"You've seen her do things?" I asked.

"We've all seen her do things, if you're just paying attention," he said. Then he looked down at his empty mug of coffee. "I'm not sure what I can do to help you. Unless you have something else for me, may I please open my shop back up to business?"

I looked at Audrey, but she just shrugged.

"He's being honest," Houdini said to all of us. "So far as I can tell. Which is, to be fair, quite far."

Titus visibly startled, and went pale. Then he leaned forward on his toes, but slowly, and only just enough to see past the end of his own counter. Down to where Houdini had been sitting there the entire time.

Houdini, whom Titus had only ever known as a little rat terrier chihuahua, and one that had always taken a vocal dislike to him every time he had so much as walked by the door of Agatha's teashop. The teashop was now Audrey's, and as far as Titus knew, Houdini was now my dog.

But I could tell by the shocked expression that was not showing any sign of leaving Titus's face that, for the first time ever, he had heard Houdini's voice inside his head.

Heard it, and known where it had come from.

But had no idea exactly what it meant.

"Greetings, Titus," Houdini said to him, even as his doggy self sat back and scratched briefly at the back of one ear.

"Hello, Houdini," Titus said, and swallowed hard. "You are... that is, I didn't know you could... I'm not sure what I mean."

"And yet I understand you," Houdini said. "If I may extend my apologies for our earlier encounters? I fear I misjudged you. But you did have the stink of dark magic on you, thanks to your wife's dealings. I know now that was nothing you could have even known yourself. I see you better now."

"Oh," Titus said, swallowing nervously again. "Yes. Apology most certainly accepted."

Then he looked at me, his eyes still wide. I could see there all the questions racing through his mind. About who and what Houdini was, just to start.

And I could see him make the firm resolution not to ask a single one of them. Because he already knew that he didn't really want to know.

He knew a dangerous secret when it brushed up against him.

"If Houdini trusts you, that's enough for me. For now," I added with just a hint of a threat in my tone. "But we'll be back if we have more questions later."

"Yes. Absolutely," Titus said. I could tell by the way his hands gripped the edge of the counter that he was just waiting for us to leave so he could collapse into a chair. And I almost pitied him.

Deciding you didn't want to know the answers wouldn't stop the questions circling around inside your mind. At least, in my experience, that had always been true.

But I just scooped up Houdini and headed back out into the Square.

Audrey gave Titus a quick thanks for the lattes, then hustled out after me.

CHAPTER

TEN

The instant we were outside of the shop and out of earshot of Titus Bloom behind his counter, I set Houdini down on the ground. Then I deliberately loomed over him, hands on my hips as I gave him my fiercest stare.

"What exactly was that all about? All of Agatha's hard work keeping you hidden and safe from danger, and you just blow it all by talking out loud? In front of Titus Bloom?" I demanded.

I might've gotten a little shrill. To judge from the hand that Audrey put on my arm, anyway.

But Houdini just blinked up at me, unperturbed.

"I trusted him," he said simply.

"Okay, you could've just told me and Audrey that," I said. "Why tell him too?"

"I don't know," Houdini said. If it's possible for a voice in the back of your head to shrug, that's what he did just then. "It just felt like the time."

"The time for what?" I asked.

"Just... the time to let him into the circle of people who know I'm not a dog," he said.

I had too many thoughts at once at that and only managed an inarticulate splutter.

But Audrey calmly took over. "What kind of feeling are we talking about, Houdini? An intuition? A conclusion from a long mulling over of things? Something from inside you or outside you?"

Which were all really good questions. But all I could do was hope my eyes conveyed my sense of dittoing everything she had just asked.

"All those things," Houdini said, maddeningly. "It was just time. I don't know how to explain it more than that."

"What else is it going to suddenly be time for? Without warning? Taking off your collar and shaking off all of Agatha's spells?" I asked. Then I choked a little as I added, "The spells she gave her life to protect you with?"

"No, I don't think so," Houdini said, as if he didn't sense a single emotion coming from me and was only hearing the words. "I don't know how to explain it. Perhaps I should confer with the Wizard."

"Right now?" Audrey asked.

"Yes, right now," I said before Houdini could answer. "Go to the Tower. See what he says. Audrey and I will be in the salon, but if Cressida's too busy to talk to us, we'll be at the teashop. Then you can tell me what the Wizard says."

"Very well," Houdini said.

"But, Houdini, you have to tell him everything that just happened. Every bit of it. And I hope you'll tell me everything he says to you," I said.

"Of course I will," he said, blinking in surprise. "I never hide anything from you, Tabitha."

I hoped that was true. I really did.

But I still didn't trust myself to speak without choking up again. I just nodded.

And he winked out of sight, teleporting to the rug in front of the fire in the Wizard's Tower.

"Tabitha?" Audrey asked, and I realized I was blinking back hot tears.

"I just need a second," I said, brushing the back of my hand across my eyes a tad too aggressively. "I didn't see that coming. I guess I was dealing okay with the Square building escape routes. I mean, I didn't think I was. But compared to what Houdini just did, I never felt unsafe then like I do now. What was he *thinking*?"

"I think he thought just what he told us," Audrey said. "He felt that it was time. I think we just have to trust him. It's really his secret we're all keeping. The call should be his."

"Sure," I said, sniffling loudly. "Be all sensible about it."

"Well," Audrey said with the hint of a smile. "I can afford to be, can't I? You're the one who is his companion. I mean, I love him too. But I'm aware it's not remotely the same thing."

"I'm supposed to keep him safe," I said.

Then Audrey was hugging me tight. And she whispered close to my ear, "That doesn't mean you're going to lose him when he doesn't need you to be safe anymore. He's a big dragon. Bigger by the day. But he's always going to be your companion."

And that was Audrey in a nutshell. Accurately pinpointing the exact thing I was truly afraid of, even when I didn't know it myself.

"Thanks," I said, hugging her back before stepping away to clean up my face with a wad of tissue I lucked upon in one of my pockets.

Thank Violenta Court, really. She insisted every witch needed clothes with lots of pockets. I was beginning to suspect those clothes came with necessary items already stowed in those pockets. Because she just had that kind of forethought.

But her shop only existed inside the Square. Wendell Gorman would never have stopped in to see her at all. So I would have to remember to thank her later.

After I'd figured out what had happened to that prosaic man.

"Ready to talk to Cressida?" Audrey asked.

I nodded, but then frowned as I peered through the glass doors to the interior of the salon. "It looks really busy in there."

"It's always busy in there," Audrey said. "We'll just let her know we need to talk to her. I'm sure if it's at all possible, she'll find a way to make the time."

"Sure," I agreed.

We pushed inside the salon, and the sudden wash of comfortably warm—if heavily product-scented—air that greeted us made me realize just how chilly it had gotten outside. It was also a lot closer to the perfect level of humidity compared to the dry autumn day behind us. I didn't have to reach up and touch my hair to feel it getting softer. I just knew. The craziness of my curl was already responding to Cressida's magic.

It was possible that Titus hadn't been exaggerating. Cressida really did have bountiful magic. And the rest of us really didn't see it.

But I was going to make a point of noticing from now on.

Audrey and I lingered uncertainly just inside the doorway, in part because we were waiting for our eyes to adjust. But Cressida saw us there before we'd even stepped further into her domain. She was busy with a customer juggling far too many implements in just two hands. But she turned to Phoebe beside her and said something too low for either Audrey or me to hear.

Phoebe nodded, then helped her own customer to her feet. She walked the woman—still wearing her cape but with her hair under a plastic cap—to a row of hood driers. Phoebe got the woman settled into the comfortable leather chair, pulled the drier down over her head and checked the settings before stepping back. With one last word that the woman nodded to, Phoebe finally turned towards the Square door and walked over to us.

"Hi," she said with a nervous smile. "You're Tabitha Greene and Audrey Mirken, right? I know we've never met, but I'm sure I recognize you both from what people have been telling me about you. I'm Phoebe Cassio."

She shook my hand, then Audrey's, still all nervousness, although I wasn't sure why. It wasn't guilty vibes, anyway. More like she was meeting someone famous.

Which didn't make a lot of sense. Even inside the Square, neither of us were famous.

Were we?

"Pleased to meet you, Phoebe," I said.

"And welcome to the Square," Audrey added.

"We were hoping to have a minute with Cressida, if that was possible?" I asked.

"Oh," Phoebe said with a sudden flush to her pale face that made the cute scattering of freckles on her cheeks stand out all the more. "I'm not sure if that's going to work today. We're awfully busy. I only have ten minutes myself, but maybe I can help you with whatever you need?"

She trailed off hopefully, although whether she was hoping the answer was yes or no, I wasn't entirely sure.

"It's about Wendell Gorman," I said. "Did you meet him at all?"

"Oh, not really," Phoebe said. But with a smile that said she really wished the answer had been a more definitive yes.

"He was here to see Cressida, I take it?" Audrey asked.

"No, actually. He only wanted to talk to Cleopatra Manx," Phoebe said. But she dropped her voice as she said it, and turned so that she was facing us a little more directly than before. I didn't think she was trying to hide what she was saying from Cressida, though. More the cluster of customers that were all around Cressida in the two work-stations as well as the waiting area beyond.

"So it was just a brief visit when he stopped in?" Audrey asked.

"Not remotely," Phoebe said with another bright smile. "No, he came in here at least a dozen times. He asked for Cleopatra every time, and Cressida would explain all over again that she was the one in charge of the shop these days. But he never seemed to really hear her, you know? Not that he was rude about it. Quite the opposite."

She gave me half a wink, but I wanted more than a vague sense of what she was hinting at. "What's the opposite?" I asked.

"Have you seen Wendell Gorman?" she asked.

Which was weirdly phrased in the present tense. And I didn't really want to bring up the fact that I had seen him, or at least his corpse.

I was still trying to string together what I *did* want to say, when Audrey stepped in again. "I heard he was quite attractive."

And she could say that with a bit more authority this time around.

"Quite," Phoebe said. She left no doubt in our minds she thought that qualifier was a bit of an understatement.

"He never chatted you up?" Audrey guessed.

"Oh, I wish," Phoebe said, pretending to fan herself. "But no. He only had eyes for Cressida. But what eyes he had. Like that old prosaic actor Paul Newman."

"And yet he didn't think she really was in charge?" I asked.

"Well, she told him often enough, and he'd seem to get it in the end each time. But when he came back, it was like his brain reset," Phoebe said. Then she gave us a thoughtful frown. "I've been studying the prosaic world, you know. Not just cosmetology, but prosaic business practices as well. I take night classes at two schools currently."

"You have a theory?" I guessed.

"As far as the prosaic world is concerned, the Inanna Salon & Spa is still owned entirely by Cleopatra Manx. That's what the paperwork says. You know, the government bureaucracy stuff?"

"Sure," I said. As if I knew anything about that.

"Yeah, well, I think that stuff has power," Phoebe went on. "Not in and of itself. It's part of what the Square touches on, to keep us all hidden, right?"

"So you weren't speaking metaphorically," Audrey guessed. "His brain really does keep resetting. He keeps having the same encounter like it's the first time?"

"No, not exactly that," Phoebe said. "It keeps resetting that specific bit of knowledge, that he needs to speak to Cleopatra Manx because she owns this small business. But every time he comes in, he remembers meeting Cressida before. He remembers all their running jokes and every bit of personal information she's ever given him."

"Except the bit about being the current owner of the salon," I said.

"Except for that," Phoebe agreed.

"Phoebe, can you ring up Ms. Thomas? I'll take over from here," Cressida said, suddenly amongst us. Phoebe spun around to see Ms. Thomas—her updo in pristine condition with her new highlights glowing with something close to actual magic but definitely not because Cressida knew and scrupulously obeyed the rules about magic and prosaics—waiting at the tall counter with her credit card already in her hand.

"Absolutely," Phoebe said brightly, then gave Audrey and me a quick nod of farewell before rushing across the salon on her kitten heels to greet Ms. Thomas.

"I guess I know what this is about," Cressida said, crossing her arms as she looked at the two of us levelly. "I can't guess how you think I can help you, however. I told you everything I knew last night. Little as that was."

"We just had a few questions," I said. But gently. Because as stern as her body language was, and as expert as her makeup application had been, I could tell she had been crying more since we had seen her last.

But then, to my surprise, Audrey added, "And a request to try out a spell for you, if we could. Something that might cheer you up."

I was grateful that Cressida's attention was entirely on Audrey in that moment. I don't know what she would've made of my slack-jawed expression at Audrey's words.

"What sort of spell?" Cressida asked Audrey. Her features were as coldly stern as before, but there was no hiding the sudden interest in her tone.

"Just something Tabitha and I have been cooking up," Audrey said. "It creates a sort of entity, like the spirit of your business. Something you can talk to and interact with."

"Interesting," Cressida allowed. "But how is it relevant now?"

"Well, we know this is one of the last places Wendell Gorman was seen alive," Audrey said. "And as much as we want to talk to you about what you know about him, it's possible that your shop itself might know things you don't."

"I can't talk to you now, obviously," Cressida said, rolling her eyes towards the crowd behind her. "But if you stop back after dinner, I'll help you however I can."

"Great," I said.

But before I'd even gotten that word out, Cressida was raising a hand to forestall me. "Be prepared to be disappointed. I honestly don't know a thing. And I doubt my shop knows more."

"But you're curious to talk to it, aren't you?" Audrey said with a conspiratorial grin.

"A touch," Cressida admitted with just a hint of a smile of her own.

But then she dismissed us both with a nod and turned back to gesture for her next customer to take the now clean chair at the mirror.

I waited until we were once more outside on the tiled patio in the chill of the October day to grab Audrey by the arm.

"Are you sure?" I asked.

"I think it will help," Audrey said. "I was thinking about it while we were in Titus's shop, but Houdini spoke up before I could offer trying it. It might still be worth doing there."

"No, I meant, are you sure you can do this?" I asked.

"You tweaked the spell," she said. Not even a question.

"I did," I said. And decided not to tell her about the bit of a spark I had felt in that moment.

"And I did ritual meditation work last night and this morning," she told me. "And I'll do it again this afternoon, before we come back here."

"Is that going to be enough?" I asked.

She laughed. "Probably not? I've been neglecting the daily practices of a ritual magician for quite some time. But it's a start. We can at least try."

"You're thinking if Cressida is as powerful as Titus says, she can help," I guessed.

She flushed, and I realized she had been thinking exactly that.

And was glad I hadn't mentioned my moment of spark. No one was going to need what little I could chip in, clearly.

Still, I had to ask. "Do you need anything more from me?"

"No," Audrey said after a moment's thought. "I'll close up the shop a smidge early to prepare. But then I'll meet you here after dinner."

Which left my afternoon wide open. Except for the shift I was supposed to be working, helping out my uncles with unpacking and shelving some books.

A shift I was already late for.

"Sounds like a plan!" I said, and gave her one last quick hug before sprinting to the bookshop.

Sometimes, with all the mystery solving that came up around the Square, I just plain forgot I had other day-to-day responsibilities. It was a good thing my uncles were so understanding.

But there was no way I would ever let myself abuse their kindness.

And anyway, what better way to distract myself from worrying about our second attempt at that spell than by touching book after book?

The afternoon was just going to fly by.

ELEVEN

udrey and I arrived at the door to the Inanna Salon & Spa at precisely the same moment, although from different directions. Which at first I thought was odd. I came from the Square door to the Weal & Woe Bookshop, and Audrey would've had to pass it to get to the salon. That was the door we should've met each other at.

But at my quizzical look, she just cocked her thumb up over her shoulder. She had been at her apartment.

She really had closed up the teashop early.

She had an oversized tote over one shoulder, with a bulge in it that just had to be from a large glass bowl.

"Was I supposed to bring anything?" I asked.

"You mean besides the spell?" Audrey asked.

"Right," I said, patting my pockets until I found the parchment tucked away in my back pocket. I had put it there that morning, before hearing Barnardo's voice in the teashop and finding him in conversation with Steph. I hadn't given it another thought since. But although it was a little flattened, the ink had been well dry before I had squashed it and nothing had smeared into illegibility.

I knocked on the door once briskly, then opened it to let Audrey and myself inside. The interior was darker than I had ever seen it, thanks to the seasonal early sunset.

And we were technically still on daylight savings time.

But the coming darkness was a worry for a different time.

"Cressida?" I called as we tiptoed past sparkling clean workstations and over neatly swept tile floors.

"Back here," Cressida called from behind the tall counter that had been like Cleopatra's dais when she had run the shop. But before we could even approach her there, Cressida was stepping down to the main floor with a pitcher of icy cold water in her hands. "Does it matter that this is infused with cucumbers? I fished all the slices out. But nothing else in the shop is this cold."

"No, actually, I think it's perfect," Audrey said, shooting a glance my way.

"Sure," I said. Because what I didn't know about physical components for ritual spells could fill entire books.

Books I should really start reading.

But in concept, I agreed with Audrey. If she had asked Cressida to provide the water base for the spell, it should be water that was specific to this shop and its purpose. And cucumber-infused water was very much of this place.

Audrey set the bowl directly on the floor in the middle of the entire salon, perpendicular to the row of hood hairdryers and in the middle of the row of pedicure stations with their now-empty foot baths. Then she gestured for Cressida to pour in her pitcher of water.

"I haven't done anything like this since my academy days," Cressida said as she sent the water cascading down from a bit higher up than I would've tried it. But the fall of that water caught lights I didn't even see around us, making them dance in silvery circles as if reflecting off a disco ball.

"I'm pretty sure you didn't do anything like this in your academy days," Audrey said with a mischievous smile as she set a fresh tea light floating on the surface of that water. Then she gestured for me to hand her the parchment.

I hadn't had a chance to go over the changes with her before, and she didn't take the time to more than glance at them now. But the satisfied lift to her mouth as she silently spoke the syllables was enough to have me glowing with pride at her implied approval.

Then she took out her wand and began reciting the words aloud in that uncanny, deep voice of hers.

The words wended their way around and around, like the poetry was playing tag with itself. It had a rhythm that Audrey quickly found, but it wasn't exactly a song or even a chant.

Still, there was no mistaking the look on Cressida's usually impassive face. She was impressed.

The dancing silver sparkles around us seemed to gather closer, as if they too were in thrall with Audrey and her intoning voice.

But no, that wasn't what they were doing. They were dancing together, in the most elaborate of chamber dances. Then their dance grew faster and faster, and tighter and tighter.

Until they became one light, a softly radiant light that was more golden now than silver.

A light in the form of a woman kneeling before the candlelit bowl of water, occupying the quadrant that the three of us had inadvertently left empty. The figure's head was bowed over the arms that she held crossed over her chest, her hands clasping lightly at her opposite shoulders. Her long hair draped down to the floor, then spilled around her like a royal mantle.

Audrey stopped speaking the words of the spell, not suddenly as if surprised that it had worked, but on the beat, as if she had always planned to stop there.

And the figure lifted her head to look at us with eyes like living lapis lazuli, and I knew at once without being told that this was Inanna. Not the goddess.

I mean, probably not the goddess.

But Inanna, the soul of the salon.

Then she looked down at her own softly glowing fingertips and chuckled, a sound of almost childlike wonder.

"This is... interesting," she said, turning her hand over to look at the backs of her wiggling fingers. "Very interesting."

I could've gazed on her radiant beauty forever, but I had to tear my eyes away. I had to look to Audrey, to be sure she was handling this load of magic all right.

But Audrey was just kneeling opposite Inanna with a soft smile of her own. I could see weariness around her eyes that I was sure hadn't been there when we'd met outside the salon door. But she was otherwise perfectly well.

For definitions of 'perfectly well' that included possibly having the greatest day of her life.

"Welcome, Inanna," Audrey said.

"Inanna, do you know me?" Cressida asked. She moved as if she wanted to reach out and take one of the hands that were still fascinating the radiant woman, but changed her mind. Although she had to hold her hands fisted tightly together against the skirt of her minidress to fight that temptation.

Inanna slowly turned her attention from her own hands to Cressida beside her.

And it was only then that I realized that Cressida had only appeared to have been imitating Cleopatra Manx's style, in the short dresses and the long flowing locks of hair.

They had both been imitating this version if Inanna. Which, again, I didn't think was truly the Babylonian goddess. Because, first of all, how crazy would that be? To think we could summon a deity, Audrey and me?

But also, because her hair was as golden as Cressida's own, and I was pretty sure that wasn't how the Babylonian goddess would've looked.

But the gods have many masks. And so do the goddesses. And what did I really know about either?

That had definitely never been my branch of magic.

"I know you, Cressida Cade," Inanna said at length. "I have known you for some time."

But the glow of pleased happiness that lit up Cressida's face faded an instant later when Inanna asked, "But where is Cleopatra Manx?"

"Cleopatra?" Cressida repeated numbly.

"She hasn't been here in so very long, has she?" Then a flutter of confusion crossed Inanna's face, almost like a ripple crossing a pond, albeit a pond reflecting golden sunlight. "Has she?"

"No, she hasn't," Cressida said. "I own... No. I manage the shop now. Is that the better word? Manage?"

"You are my advocate in this world," Inanna said after another long moment's thought.

"Advocate, yes," Cressida said.

But Inanna was frowning again. "Ownership is power. We don't like to be under another's power."

"No, of course not," Cressida rushed to say. "I didn't mean—"

But Inanna didn't seem to hear her. "To be under Cleopatra Manx's power.... We agreed to it, of course. We consented. And we miss it now. It's gone, isn't it? That yoke to our power? We miss it."

"I'm... sorry?" Cressida ventured.

"No," Inanna said. "Don't be. We prefer your advocacy to being yoked by Cleopatra Manx."

"But you feel conflicted?" I found myself saying. I hadn't meant to interrupt what felt like a deeply personal moment between the two of them. And I really didn't mean to draw the power of those lapis lazuli eyes on me.

But I didn't attempt to take my words back. I just lifted my chin and waited for Inanna's answer.

"Conflicted. Yes," she said musingly.

"Because the transfer wasn't handled correctly?" I asked. Another guess.

But I had the feeling that Phoebe knew her stuff about how our Square interacted with the prosaic world.

Although Cressida had no idea what I was talking about, and made no attempt to hide her shock and irritation as she glared at me across the candlelit bowl.

Inanna mused on my words for a moment, but then nodded. "Yes. Something was left incomplete. Something small, but important. I can feel it. I'm not yet free. I want to give myself totally to Cressida Cade. I love Cressida Cade. But something is holding me back."

Cressida started to speak, but Audrey reached out and clasped her hand tightly.

"We know how to fix that," Audrey said. She was speaking to Inanna, but she was looking at Cressida.

Who heard her and relented with a nod.

"Inanna," I said. "You know everything that happens inside the Square, don't you?"

"Only my part of it," she told me. "The rest is merely echoes. Confusing overlapping echoes. But I know my domain."

"But you sounded confused before, about whether or not Cleopatra Manx has been here?" I said. "You know that Cleopatra Manx killed a beloved matagot here in the Square, and she nearly killed one of the resident magicians as well. Barnardo Daley."

"Yes, I know," Inanna said in her maddeningly slow way. "That was why Cleopatra Manx was sent away. That was when I started to move from under Cleopatra's thumb into a partnership with Cressida. She left me such lovely offerings, and spoke to me even though I was powerless to answer her in like words."

Cressida flushed deeply, equal parts embarrassed that Audrey and I knew she had been effectively talking to herself in her first lonely days running the salon by herself, but also pleased that the salon had always heard her. Her instincts had been spot on.

But I still had more to say to Inanna, so I pressed on before Cressida could speak whatever was in her heart.

"Cleopatra has been here since she was sent away, though. Hasn't she?" I asked.

Inanna chewed at her radiantly glowing lip. "Time is hard. Place is better. She has been here."

"Okay, but it's really important that you think about the time too," I said. "Was Cleopatra here recently? Secretly? Like she was sneaking around when Cressida wasn't here?"

Audrey gave me a little nod, as if agreeing that focusing on the characteristics that Cleopatra's recent visits must have had if they had happened was the smart play.

I guess I just understood the way days could pass in a blur. Mine had for a month. I couldn't have given any sequence to the events of those days, not even if pressed.

I doubted the spirit of the salon could either. Especially if it, unlike me, hadn't even started out with any kind of concept of time.

But the glowing form of Inanna was quickly nodding in answer to my words, and the color washed out of Cressida's face as she realized what all that meant.

"She's been here? But she's under house arrest? How could she...?" But not even Cressida could maintain any incredulity at the actions of her former mentor, the woman she had looked up to for so many years as she served as her loyal apprentice. "Of course she did," she concluded bitterly, then bit down hard on her own lip to stop further words.

"Was she meeting anyone inside here?" I asked Inanna. "When she was being secretive? Was she meeting someone in the dark?"

"Meeting? No, there was no meeting," Inanna said. "There was just passing through. She moved through me to get in and out of the Square."

The Square. The one place she absolutely wasn't supposed to be inside of. Aside from the fact that, being under house arrest, the *only* place she was supposed to be inside of was the Manx family condo in Manhattan.

But, to my surprise, Inanna wasn't done speaking. "The man came looking for her. So many times."

"The man? Do you mean Wendell Gorman?" I asked.

"The handsome man," Inanna said, and her glow kicked up a notch.

And Cressida was blushing furiously herself.

I really hadn't gotten a good look at him. Not that I had seen him at his best, being several hours dead and all.

"He came during the day," Audrey said as if stating a mere fact.

But Inanna was shaking her head before Audrey had even finished speaking. "No, he came during the night as well. Always looking for Cleopatra. Looking and looking and never finding."

"Why?" I asked.

But Inanna just blew out a long breath that seemed to take a great deal of her inner glow with it.

And I realized the spell was fading.

The tea light in the center of the bowl of water was starting to sputter out. I shot a questioning glance at Audrey, but she gave me a quick shake of her head. No, lighting another candle would not extend the spell. It was coming to an end.

"I don't know why," Inanna said even as she started to fade away. "I don't know why. I tried my best. I tried to bring him to Cressida. But the pull in him for Cleopatra was so strong. So strong. So strong..."

The last syllable hung in the air, like a glitch in a digital recording.

And then she was gone, and the three of us were alone in the total darkness of the salon.

But out of the dark, I heard Cressida suck in a shaky breath before saying, "Thank you. I don't know if that helped you at all with whatever you're hoping to find. But thank you both. That was a true gift."

"If Phoebe needs help bringing your prosaic business filings up to date, let me know. My boyfriend Liam is a prosaic, and he'd be happy to help," Audrey said.

"Yes. Yes, I'll do that," Cressida said.

That would make it official, and it would please the spirit of her shop to have that last formality completed.

But honestly, there was no question in any of our minds. This salon belonged to Cressida Cade now.

And they were both so happy with each other. No wedding had ever touched me that deeply.

I couldn't wait to try that spell again.

TWELVE

I wasn't exactly surprised when Audrey begged off the minute we left the salon. She wasn't looking as wrecked as she had after the first time we'd tried that spell, but she had still had a far busier day than I had. And I had been hauling books around.

But I was surprised that when I got back to my nook in the bookshop, there was still no sign of Houdini. I went up to my bedroom, but he wasn't there either.

If he were in trouble, I would know. Someone would've told me. The Wizard or Steph or.... someone.

Right?

They had to. I didn't have enough magic on my own to get back inside the Tower. Not without Houdini.

In the end, I didn't really have any other choice. I took out my phone and sent Steph a text.

Which he responded to at once, only not with a text back. In between one blink and the next in the dark interior of my bedroom, he was just there beside me.

He had a very flustered energy, like I had just caught him mid conversation. So much so for half a second I wondered if I had pulled him to me with my own power rather than him teleporting himself to my side.

Could I do that?

But before I could apologize or even ask, he threw an arm around me and in the next blink of an eye, I was standing with him on the faded rug in front of the Wizard's fire.

And I saw, to my relief, that Houdini was already there. He was curled up on the Wizard's lap, his nose tucked under his back leg, clearly profoundly asleep.

But he and the Wizard weren't alone in the Tower's library. Sheriff Jane MacMorris and Deputy Eric Fluellen were there too. The sheriff was in the chair I usually sat in, the one directly opposite of the Wizard's own chair. But the deputy was further from the fire, in the shadows by the bookshelves. He was tapping away at the tablet in his hands in a manner I was all too familiar with.

The two of them were the entire police force in our part of Minneapolis. And they were thoroughly overworked. I knew without asking that the deputy was busy triaging all the other work that was coming their way while the sheriff focused all the attention she could on whatever she was discussing with the Wizard.

Said discussion being what I had inadvertently pulled Steph away from.

But I didn't dare interrupt their conversation to even whisper an apology to Steph. Although when I looked up at him, I could see that apology was entirely unnecessary. He understood. In fact, he looked almost chagrined. Like he had forgotten that I might be an interested party in this conversation before I had texted him. Or, at least, that I might have been terribly worried about Houdini.

"That's just the thing, Volumnia *can't* be sure," the sheriff was saying to the Wizard. "And without that assurance, we can't make this our problem."

Then she started to get up from her chair, and at the sight of her moving, the deputy started to put his tablet away.

And I realized I had just missed a lot, and I didn't exactly know what was going on. But I felt the absolute conviction that I couldn't just let them walk away.

That would mean case closed on Wendall Gorman. And they didn't even know what I knew yet.

"Wait," I said, flailing my arms as if they might have missed seeing me standing there between them and the library's main light source.

Houdini heard my voice and stirred enough to open a single eye and peer out at me. But he stayed where he was under the Wizard's gently stroking hand.

"Miss Greene," the sheriff said, hooking her thumbs on her belt that, given her large power lifter frame, was all too reminiscent of a wrestling prize belt. "I'm sure you're filled with questions. You usually are. But young Steph there will have to catch you up. I simply haven't the time."

"No questions," I said, although in fact I had a million of them. "I just need to tell you what Audrey and I have learned."

"Yes, I understand you were grilling people," the sheriff said wearily. "You know, if there are suspects to be questioned, my deputy and I have the authority to conduct those interviews. The *sole* authority."

"I know," I said. "This wasn't so much a suspect as a witness, and I don't think it's anything you would've thought to question. Respectfully," I added, all too belatedly.

But Deputy Fluellen caught something that the sheriff missed. "Any*thing*?" he said with a raised eyebrow.

The sheriff just sighed and crossed her arms, as much as she was willing to do to indicate that she would hear me out.

"Audrey and I did a spell that brought the part of the Square that is the Inanna Salon & Spa to life," I said.

The Wizard's eyebrows shot up at that, but he said nothing, not wanting to interrupt.

"I don't understand," the sheriff said.

"The spells that protect the Square are in turn fed by the residents of the Square," Steph said from behind me. "That gives the network of those spells something very like sentience. It sounds like Tabitha has worked out a way to tease out that semblance of sentience and... well, ask it pertinent questions."

"And get answers that are usable in court?" the sheriff asked skeptically.

"I have no idea about the legality of it all," I admitted. "I'm just telling you that the Inanna Salon & Spa is very aware of the presence of Cleopatra Manx. Because she was once the owner, and in the prosaic world still is. They are still bound together. And the salon told me unequivocally that Cleopatra Manx has been using that shop to get in and out of the Square. Like, recently."

"She's under house arrest," the sheriff said with total confidence. "We've already checked up on her. She's not left her confinement since she was placed there a month ago."

"Says who? Her family?" I asked.

The sheriff ran the tip of her tongue over her bottom lip, as if that gesture could lend her more patience. Then she said, "Those were the terms of her house arrest. She was remanded to the custody of the Manx family."

"Violating the terms would have very strict penalties for them," Deputy Fluellen put in.

"If they're caught," I said.

"Which they won't be on the word of a shop," the sheriff said. "Especially not one that can't speak testimony in court. Which, I'm guessing, it can't."

"There might be a way," I said, although I could feel Steph behind me resisting the urge to shake his head. He knew more about the spells of the Square than I did, but I wasn't willing to concede defeat just yet.

"It really doesn't matter," the sheriff said, signaling for the deputy to move closer to her side. "The case is closed. Volumnia is already preparing the body to be moved to the prosaic world."

"Volumnia knows what killed him?" I asked, turning to look at Steph.

"No," he said.

"And it doesn't matter," the sheriff said. "We know he was killed outside the Square and then his corpse was moved inside. Ergo, not our jurisdiction."

"Seriously? You haven't ruled out that he was killed by magic and then brought into the Square? You know, like the last dead body we had around here?"

I knew I had gone too far. Even before I felt Steph's hands on my shoulders, I knew I was pressing too hard and too angrily.

But I couldn't back off.

"That all sorted itself out in the end," the sheriff said, not quite defensively. "Her case was closed to the satisfaction of the prosaic police force, and her killer most certainly found justice."

"Because the faeries intervened," I said. "Is that going to happen again this time?"

"I don't have time for this," the sheriff said, more to the Wizard than to me. Which just made me all the angrier.

But then she and the deputy were gone, and anything else I wanted to say to her had to just die on my tongue, unuttered.

"Houdini explained to me what he did in the coffeeshop," the Wizard said, giving me conversation-changing whiplash.

"I wish he would explain it to me, then," I said, rubbing at my forehead.

"I did explain it to you," Houdini said sleepily. "I felt it was time."

"And that's what he told you?" I asked the Wizard.

"It's perfectly understandable," the Wizard said.

I just gaped at them both.

"Houdini did promise to tell you first, the next time he feels like the time has come for some drastic change to the status quo," Steph told me.

"Yes, I promised," Houdini said, then promptly went back to sleep.

"I guess I'll have to be satisfied with that, then," I said.

Not satisfied at all.

"This spell of yours sounds very interesting," the Wizard said even as he resumed stroking the fur of Houdini's curled back.

"Yes, well," I said, letting my upset feelings deflate a little.

Then I gave him and Steph a detailed description of the spell, and how it worked, and what it had revealed.

To my relief, they were less dismissive of the implications than the sheriff and deputy had been.

"If the salon says Cleopatra has been here, I think it's very like she has been here," Steph said, and the Wizard nodded his agreement.

"But what does it mean? If she had killed that man and brought him inside through the salon, surely Inanna would've just said so? But all she said was that Cleopatra had been there, and the man had been looking for her, but that he had never found her there."

"It is certainly always a possibility that your Inanna was confused," the Wizard said. "But I doubt it. Even if Cleopatra brought the body of that man through the salon hidden inside of something, I suspect the salon would've sensed him. From what you said, it sounded like it was sensitive to his presence."

"It sounded like the salon had a bit of a crush," Steph said, amused.

"You don't think it could be faerie magic again? Another cocoon?" I asked.

"No," the Wizard said with a firm shake of his head. "No, not after the spellwork Steph and I endeavored to do since. No faerie magic inside the Square. We would know at once. By the way whatever faerie magic-infused thing bounced off the spells and was ejected back out into the prosaic world."

"Well, that doesn't sound ideal," I grumbled.

But then I heard a voice speaking from behind me. A voice I had never heard before in my life, but a voice I knew in my soul.

"No, not ideal. And yet, heartening to hear. Isn't it?"

And then he was brushing past me, so close that the folds of his coat with all of its brightly shining brass buttons brushed against the side of my jeans.

It was my father. I was in the same room as my father.

And even though I knew that the Tower was the safest place in the world, I had never felt less safe than I did in that moment.

Even with Steph's hand finding its way into mine and giving it a hard squeeze, I still felt so very, very unsafe.

And that man, that man who was my father, was between me and Houdini. And I liked that least of all.

CHAPTER

THIRTEEN

My father had once been inside my mind. Not the way Houdini's voice was. No, when my father was in there, it was far more intrusive. It had been completely overwhelming. He had never spoken to me. He had only been inside my very being, crushing me.

So I'm not exactly sure why his actual voice was instantly familiar to me. It was possible some lost part of my memory contained a moment we were together when I was very young, and I had heard him speak then. And it had left such an impression on me that I remembered it still after all these years of not remembering it at all.

But I couldn't say for sure. I had more memories of my days before my first magical academy now than I had before I'd come to my Square. But that wasn't saying a lot.

Before I had come to the Square, I hadn't even remembered I had two uncles. I hadn't remembered a single thing that had happened to me before the very traumatic testing process that had led to the conclusion that followed me throughout my academy days: that I had no magic to speak of and even less control.

Maybe it was more than his voice I remembered. Maybe it was just his presence. It had the same overwhelming, stifling feeling I had felt before on a street corner in Geneva, and again on a condo-lined street by the river in St. Anthony a few blocks away.

I was very glad that Steph was there with me. His hand in mine lent me the strength I needed.

Because that man, that odious man, was still between me and Houdini. And I couldn't just dart around him to snatch up my dog.

No, the most important thing in that moment was that Benvolio Ward not notice Houdini at all, if that were even possible. I absolutely couldn't draw attention to him.

But it was so hard.

I had never seen my father before with my own eyes, not even in a photograph. But I recognized his look at once from the description that Liam had given to me the month before. Tall, like my brother Mercutio. Full head of silver hair, although Liam had neglected to describe the natural wave to that hair that replicated a pompadour without any product being involved.

He was standing with his back to me now as he spoke with the Wizard, but I could just see the wire frame of his glasses. Round, green lenses. That was what Liam had told me. Although that sounded so much like an affectation, like a fashion accessory, that I wouldn't be surprised if they were blue or violet or even rose-colored now.

Long, tailored coat covered with buttons. I had noticed that already. The way it billowed around him like some dark lord's cloak, it was a little hard to miss.

It kind of looked like it was still billowing around him, actually. Like there was a fan blowing on him but not on any of the rest of us.

Perhaps it was magical, like the multicolored cloak Steph used to teleport across the world.

Certainly something must have assisted him. It was impossible to enter the Tower without the Wizard's express permission. And I really didn't think the Wizard had given my father the same open invitation to come and go at will that Houdini and I enjoyed.

At the moment, the Wizard was still lounging deep in the embrace of his wing-backed chair, one hand idly stroking the no longer dozing Houdini.

Houdini was looking straight at me with wide, terrified eyes. But he clearly didn't dare try to talk to me. Technically, he could make himself heard by only the people he chose to hear him, even inside a room crowded with people he didn't want to hear.

But neither of us wanted to risk that in the presence of my father. He might not hear Houdini's words—*might* not—but he still might sense something.

And we didn't want to risk it.

"You could've brought all this up with the sheriff and her deputy when they were here, you know," the Wizard was saying mildly to my father. "You just missed them. Although I do suspect that was intentional."

"My dear Fortinbras," my father said with a warm chuckle. "You can scarcely be surprised if I choose not to rub elbows with such folk when I can avoid it."

"Hm," was all the Wizard said.

But I was sneaking a glance up at Steph's face. His eyes met mine with the same surprise I was feeling.

The Wizard had a name? An actual name?

And it was *Fortinbras*?

"But we don't have to pretend like our local authorities are undertaking any sort of investigation in this matter," my father went on. Then he swept a questioning hand over to the empty chair across from the Wizard.

The Wizard nodded his consent, and my father arranged the folds of that coat around him, settling into the faded wing-backed chair with gentle grace. As if he feared it might break beneath him.

He was still wearing the green-tinted lenses. They weren't

terribly dark, but the wire frames were so reflective it was still impossible to see his eyes. What color they were.

Which way he was looking.

He picked an invisible bit of lint off the knee of his pinstriped trousers before folding his hands in a way that made the single silver band on his ring finger catch the light. No gem stone, no engraving, just a simple band of silver. Rather like a wedding band.

"No," he finally went on, "We are all well aware that there is only one source of investigations into the goings-on inside this Square, and it isn't the authorities, is it?"

"That's why you're here?" the Wizard asked mildly.

"Indeed. I can only assume that I am on your suspect list. Not that I take offense. I know how the world works, and how it sees me. But I thought I'd save you the trouble of sending your young apprentice to summon me and come myself just as soon as my shop was closed for the day."

"You're here to answer questions?" Steph asked, and I fought the urge to shrink behind him. To get out of the line of sight before my father glanced over our way.

But even though I steeled myself and stood tall out in the open, it didn't matter. Even with those glasses on, I could tell my father only had eyes for Steph.

The wrinkling of his nose was also sufficient communication of his feelings at being interrupted in the middle of a conversation between grownups.

I felt Steph's whole body tense through our joined hands. But he just pressed on. "All our questions?"

"Well, within reason," Benvolio Ward said with a chuckle. "I'm rather surprised you didn't call on me much earlier."

"Why?" I asked. Then immediately wished I could take it back. I didn't want his attention on me.

But he just shifted his gaze from the Wizard to Steph and back again. As if he wasn't sure which of the two of them had just spoken.

Like I was invisible or something.

"Why would we have questioned you sooner?" the Wizard asked at last.

"Surely you already know that man was inside the Square searching for Cleopatra Manx?" my father said, sounding like he'd be very surprised if the answer was no.

"We are aware of that, yes," the Wizard said.

I bit down on my lip, hard. Steph looked down at me as if he'd felt that happen through our joined hands, just like I'd felt his earlier emotional state. Then he said, "Actually, we're aware that Wendell Gorman was looking to meet Cleopatra Manx at her salon. So far, the evidence we've gathered only says he wanted to meet her, not that he succeeded in finding her. And more, the evidence indicates he was killed outside of the Square and then his body was brought inside. It seems highly unlikely he was ever inside the Square while still alive."

"Highly unlikely, you say?" my father said with undisguised disdain. "Perhaps it was highly unlikely. But highly unlikely things happen. And around here, more often than they should."

"What are you saying?" Steph demanded.

"I know the man was inside the Square," my father said, but his eyes were on the Wizard again. "He came to my apartment."

"Your apartment?" Steph repeated.

"The apartment Cleopatra Manx acquired for you," the Wizard said.

"Exactly," my father said.

"But how would a prosaic know that? There are no records of such transactions. And anyone he would ask who might even know it was ever hers at all would surely know it was only hers for a matter of days," the Wizard said.

"And yet, there he was. At my doorstep. Looking for her."

Those last three words came out dripping with such disdain, I wondered just what Cleopatra Manx had done to earn his ire. It had to be more than flubbing the job of killing Barnardo's matagot Miss Snooty Cat. Because Miss Snooty Cat had indeed died.

Cleopatra had just gotten caught rather than skating away scot-free.

For definitions of being caught that involved being held under house arrest by her apparently quite permissive family.

"When was this?" the Wizard asked, again in his mildest of tones. He was still stroking the visibly trembling Houdini.

"The very night he disappeared," Benvolio Ward said, leaning back into the wings of the chair and crossing his legs in a thoroughly relaxed and unbothered posture. "Hence my surprise when no one came to ask me about it."

"So, you were the last person to see Wendell Gorman alive?" I asked.

Again, he acted like it was Steph who had spoken, not leaning forward enough to even make eye contact from around the wing of the chair before saying, "No. Obviously, the last person to see the prosaic alive was the magician who killed him."

"You know it was a magician, then?" I said. If he was going to pretend I wasn't there, I could at least use that to my advantage and get some answers.

"It seems the most logical conclusion, but far be it from me to direct your work."

I couldn't see his face. He didn't seem to be looking my way. If anything, he seemed to be facing the Wizard again.

But something about the way he said the words "your work," I just knew they were directed at me.

He almost sounded... proud?

"Shortly after retiring to my apartment at the end of a long day of running my shop alone, just as I was about to settle in with a book and a brandy, there was a knock at my door," my father said. "You can imagine my surprise, seeing a prosaic at my door. And not one of the local pet prosaics, either. This man I had never seen before in my life. But he was asking to speak to Cleopatra Manx. And didn't quite believe me when I told him she wasn't there. That she no longer owned the apartment in question and therefore wouldn't *be* in, so there was no point in him returning later to call again. No, he didn't take it well at all."

"Threatening, was he?" Steph asked.

"Hm? No," my father said from the depths of his chair. "No, I would say more he was at the end of his rope. He was... distraught. I thought perhaps he had wandered into the Square through some weak spot in the spellwork, quite by accident, and perhaps now found himself trapped like a rat in a maze. I *did* offer to walk him back out, but he ran away before I could even reach for my coat. I had just concluded he must have reached safety when I heard Cressida Cade call out. And, well, I didn't bother to go down. I could put the pieces together well enough without seeing the end result for myself."

"You knew he was dead?" I asked.

He stirred a little at that, as if for a moment he had almost been tempted to lean forward and actually look at me.

But that quickly subsided, and again it was only his warm voice that reached me. "Someone must have lured him inside, to his detriment. If I had invited him in, perhaps he would've survived the night. But alas, I didn't think you had any of the bad sorts of young magicians in this neighborhood. I guess I know better now."

"You think he was the victim of young magicians with bad intentions *hazing* a prosaic?" I asked, completely incredulous.

It was really hard to tell, but I was pretty sure back in the shadows of the depths of that chair, he just shrugged.

"There are groups that attract such young magicians in some neighborhoods, yes," the Wizard said. "But that would never be tolerated here in the Square."

"You wouldn't allow it, of course, Fortinbras," my father said almost slyly.

But the Wizard was shaking his head. "No, the Square itself wouldn't tolerate it. You do realize that in addition to the finest structural magicians of their age, the groundwork for this place was heavily influenced by the spells of Agatha Mirken?"

"That has been the rumor," my father allowed.

"I assure you, it is no rumor," the Wizard said.

My father said nothing for a very long time. Behind me, the log on the fire cracked loudly, followed by a soft hiss as a fresh shower of sparks fell to ash.

Then my father grudgingly said, "I see."

And that was all.

But that was enough. Those two syllables were filled with enough grim acceptance that I finally felt my body untensing. I was releasing tension I hadn't even realized I had been holding.

And I had been holding it since my father had moved in.

But I had heard it. In those two short words, I had heard it.

I had heard my father realize that, whatever his plans had been when he'd come to the Square, he knew now they would come to nothing.

The spells Agatha Mirken had woven were going to last far beyond her lifetime. And they would keep protecting us all.

Not even he, with all his dark power, could change that.

CHAPTER

FOURTEEN

No one spoke for the longest time. It was like we were all absorbing the full weight of my father's last two words. Even my father.

Another log on the fire cracked, then snapped in two. The halves settled into embers in another hissing shower of sparks.

And Houdini jumped lightly down from the Wizard's lap to trot across the room. He didn't even have to paw at my knee to ask to be picked up. By the time he reached me, I was already bending over to scoop him up into my arms.

I buried my nose in the fur at the back of his neck and he made a sound that was almost like a purr. Perhaps he was spending too much time with Barnardo's kitten, Sia.

But I didn't tease him about it at all. I rather felt like purring myself, having him back in my arms.

My father, again, was the one who broke the silence. And his voice, which before had been pitched to fill the library, was now directed so closely to just the Wizard that Steph and I had to strain to hear his words.

"That doesn't make you as safe as you'd like to think," he said. "I heard about what happened with Nell Bloom. A mortal magician with no great claim to power was enough to bring down Agatha Mirken. Perhaps her power as a witch was always overstated."

"There is more to that entire situation than you know," the Wizard said.

"Oh, I'm quite certain of that fact," my father said. "I would even venture to say I'd give credence to the other rumor, that a pact with an entity from the under realms was truly the cause of Agatha's downfall. But I believe my point still stands."

I wanted to argue... something. I'm not sure exactly what was about to come out of my mouth. But Steph squeezed my hand in silent signal, and I bit my tongue.

And nuzzled Houdini closer. Because the real reason that Agatha hadn't had the power to fight Nell Bloom and the being she had made a pact with was that she had expended it all protecting my little guy.

But I had apparently made enough of an attempt at speech before that hand squeeze that I had drawn my father's attention. Kind of. He half-glanced our way.

But Steph still felt like it would be best to step in and redirect Benvolio Ward's attention. "Your point still stands? That her power was overstated?" he asked.

"That you're not as safe as you think you are," my father said. "I saw all the fresh warding you wove in last month. I would judge this neighborhood quite airtight against the influence of faerie magic. A rare but dangerous thing. Excellent work by you both." He clapped his hands a few times, not quite sarcastically.

"Rare enough for no one to think we needed protection from it before," the Wizard said. "Rare enough we likely won't need to be protected from it again in the future. And yet, now we are."

"Yes, as I said, I understand the motivation. And, again, the work was top-notch," my father said drily.

"And yet?" Steph said.

"Well, a prosaic was wandering around the Square. And not one of the pet prosaics. A stranger. Surely that is more what these protections are meant to prevent happening. And yet, happen it did."

I bristled—a lot—at the word "pet." I had let it pass the first time. But I had no doubt the "pet prosaic" he kept referencing, however obliquely, was Liam Kelly. Who lived inside the Square. And probably also my uncle Frank, who had been married to my magical uncle for decades but would always be a prosaic as well.

And it wasn't too crazy a thought that my father meant those words to carry a little menace. It wasn't an explicit threat, not in the presence of the Wizard.

But it wasn't *not* a threat.

"Perhaps I should speak more plainly," my father said, sounding downright amused now.

"Please do," the Wizard said, not the least bit offended.

"I am offering my services. I don't think I need to present you with my credentials for you to appreciate what I'm offering," my father said.

"No, it's very well known you were the finest ritual magician of your age," the Wizard said.

"*Am,*" my father corrected.

"Of course. You *are* the finest ritual magician of your age," the Wizard said with an indulgent smile.

"That I've left the cutthroat world of magical politics aside for the quiet life of a shopkeeper doesn't diminish my power," my father said darkly. "You of all wizards should know that. You've withdrawn from society almost completely within the walls of your precious Tower."

"That's—" I started to object, but to my surprise, it wasn't Steph that cut me off this time before I could say too much. It was the Wizard.

Although, being the Wizard, he did it in the mildest way possible. He merely talked over me.

"I shall consider your kind offer, Benvolio. And we, of course, thank you for stopping by to give us your witness testimony. That was most helpful," he said, even as he struggled to get up from his chair.

My father leapt agilely to his feet to extend his hands towards the Wizard. But the Wizard just waved him off, preferring to leverage himself out of the depths of his cushioned seat by the strength of his bony hands on the faded arms of the chair.

It was not a comfortable experience, standing by to watch that wobbly process. But in the end, the Wizard was on his feet.

Which put his eyes at about the level of the center of my father's chest. But the Wizard was as unbothered by the height difference as he was by anything else. He just looked up at the green lenses of my father's glasses for all the world with the air that he was looking just a little bit down at him.

"Yes, Stephanos and I shall take your kind offer under careful consideration. We will be in touch."

Then he patted my father's arm in what could only be read as a dismissive manner and toddled off towards the staircase. We could just hear him mumbling something about tuna fish as he departed.

Benvolio Ward stood there for a long moment, as if uncertain what he wanted to do next. But in the end, he just turned to Steph and gave him a tight little bow.

And that, too, read as dismissive, as much as it was meant to be a gesture of respect in every culture I knew of.

"You know where to call on me when you decide to accept my offer," he said.

I wasn't sure if Steph planned to answer that comment at all, but before he even would've had the chance to, my father was gone.

We were alone in the library with the dying fire.

"Hungry?" Steph finally said, far too brightly after everything that had just transpired. But I could scarcely blame him for wanting to change the mood.

"Tuna fish sandwiches do sound lovely," I said, still snuggling Houdini close.

Steph led the way down the spiral staircase, past the levels of the

Tower with personal bedrooms and workshops and other things, all the way down to the sunken stone floor of the kitchen.

The Wizard was deep in the process of making the sandwiches, just sliding a mound of diced pickles off the cutting board and into the bowl filled with uncanned fish and slick, shiny scoops of mayonnaise. He added a long squirt of mustard from a yellow bottle, then stirred it all together with a spoon in one hand while adding a pinch of salt and several pinches of pepper with the other.

"Chips?" Steph said with a tone of weary fondness.

"Naturally," the Wizard said, indicating one of the heavy wooden cupboards with a tip of his bald head.

"My father seems to assume you're going to say yes," I said as I hovered uselessly with Houdini in my arms.

"That's probably a safe assumption," Steph said as he returned to the table with a can of stacked potato chips.

"But you can't just let him mess around with the spells that protect us. Can you?" I asked. Maybe a little too shrilly.

"He's not wrong," the Wizard said as he sliced a loaf of LeBeau's best sandwich bread into thin but still soft slices. "Nell Bloom should never have been able to hide what she was doing from us. Faerie magic cocoons should not have slid through our protections without us even being aware. Wendell Gorman should not have been wandering the interior of the Square unescorted."

"Do you really think he was lured in here?" I asked.

"Is there another explanation?" the Wizard asked.

"That my father is lying?" I said.

"No," the Wizard said with a sad shake of his head. "No, he wasn't lying."

Houdini lifted his head from my shoulder to look at me and said, "No, I don't think he was lying either. He might not have been telling us everything, but he wasn't telling us anything that wasn't true."

"There is an upside to letting him help us as well," the Wizard said, stopping to count the number of slices before adding one more, then cleaning the crumbs from the knife before putting it back on the magnetic rack.

"What's that?" I asked.

"If he weaves his magic into the magic already part of the Square, he will be invested in this place in a way he can't just ignore or walk away from or even pervert to his own ends," Steph said. "The thing about the Square that mimics sentience, it will flow into him even as his magic flows into it. And I promise you, the Square's sense of self is far stronger."

"It's not going to turn him from villain to hero," I said skeptically.

"Well—" Steph started to say.

But the Wizard was quicker. "Your father is not a villain, Tabitha. He's not evil. He's just ambitious."

"That's just what's worrying me about him," I insisted. "He's ambitious. But, for all intents and purposes, he seems to have set all the usual ambitions aside. He broke with his own family when my brother and I were born. No matter the official line of descent, he won't be the head of the family, ever. Right?"

"I believe that's already been written in blood by his grandfather, yes," the Wizard agreed. "Your father will never be the titular head of the Ward family."

"And he gave up on politics," I said. "To be a shopkeeper? I don't think so. But what else is there left for his ambitious nature to pursue?"

"I would think it was obvious," the Wizard said, far more quietly than he usually spoke.

"What do you mean?" Steph asked, pausing in his work of distributing chips to the plates on the table to give his mentor his unwavering attention.

"Perhaps you only heard the condescension in his tone and missed the import of his word choice," the Wizard said as he dolloped the tuna fish mixture onto the bread slices, then spread them flat with the back of the spoon.

"He wants what you have," I guessed. "He wants to be a wizard in a tower, pursuing his own research."

The Wizard smiled at me, pleased in a way none of my academy teachers ever had been when I had provided the correct answer to one of their questions.

Me, the girl with no magic.

But that wasn't true, was it?

No, in fact, it was the single thing bothering me about my father's theoretical plans.

"The thing he wants to study in his tower, though, is forbidden magic," I said.

"But surely by now we've all agreed that forbidding the study of chaos is a detriment to all of us," the Wizard said. "Not just you few chaos magicians who still emerge among us from time to time. All of our magic is lessened for not including all of it in our studies. All our lives are lessened when any one of us is told that their being is simply not one we'll allow to exist."

"So you're saying my father is right?" I asked.

"It's not all of one thing or of another," the Wizard said, sounding a little irritated now. "That's just the problem. You are not raw chaos. Raw chaos does not exist. You have within you bits of order magic as well. We all do. We're all a mix of everything, more of some things and precious little of others. But none of us are complete without understanding everything we are and everything we could be."

I didn't know how to answer that. I felt like the philosophical was getting a little too mixed up in what was deeply personal to me. And I didn't like my personal conundrums being smacked down by big philosophical issues. At all.

Not even if it was the Wizard delivering the smack downs.

But then Steph said, "I think we can all agree that chaos and order are magical paths that should be studied. No one here thinks otherwise. The real issue is, is Benvolio Ward really the magician that should be putting himself at the forefront of this research? Is *that* good for anybody? Besides, possibly, Benvolio himself?"

I gave Steph my most radiantly thankful look while the Wizard busied himself with putting the top bread on each of the sandwiches. He cut each into a pair of neat triangles before adding them to the plates with stacked chips that Steph had arranged within his reach.

Then he stood back, sucking a bit of mayonnaise from the side of his thumb, looking for all the world like he was admiring his work on those sandwiches.

Then he pulled the thumb from his mouth to say, "Perhaps not. But he's not wrong about the Square. It is in distress. We all feel it."

"Can he really help? Or will he just make it worse?" I asked.

"That," the Wizard said as he pushed plates towards me and then Steph, "is what the Square will decide."

I ate my sandwich in silence. But I couldn't erase the image in my mind of all the emergency exits the Square had been building for us.

Something was coming. And just because my father had been here for a month now didn't mean the thing that was on its way wasn't still him.

He just hadn't acted yet.

FIFTEEN

After finishing that sandwich, I had a strong urge to see my uncles. I needed hugs from the only real family I had ever known, and I needed them kind of now.

But also, I could sense a lot of thoughts running through Steph's mind as he picked at his own sandwich. I didn't need him to tell me that he needed time alone with the Wizard. As bothered as I was by what the Wizard had just said, I had only known the Wizard for a few months.

Steph had been working with him very closely for years. And before I had moved into the Square, I don't think he really got outside of the Tower much. The Wizard had been his entire world from the day he left the academy until the day I dragged him to tea and scones at Audrey's teashop and forced him into fellowship with the two of us, and then Liam, and eventually even Barnardo.

I think he was better for it. I think *he* thought he was better for it, too.

But that didn't really change how important his relationship with the Wizard was. And I could tell that the Wizard choosing not to be antagonistic to Benvolio Ward was something Steph was having a really hard time accepting.

I also kind of knew that after the emotional discussion was over, the two of them would get into the logistics of what they'd be doing next to the spells that protected the Square. And they really didn't need me there for that.

So after my sandwich and chips were gone, I kissed Steph goodbye, mumbled something about having a good night to the Wizard, then scooped up Houdini and let his power take us back to the bookshop.

But rather than the kitchen of my uncles' apartment, when I opened my eyes I found we were standing on the little porch outside the French window of my attic bedroom.

Before I could even ask Houdini why we were there—was he just that tired?—I saw something moving in the darkness of my bedroom.

I recognized that body language, even in dark silhouette. My brother. Again. Only this time inside.

But before my annoyance could really build into anger, I realized he wasn't alone.

There was a figure with him, slumped on the floor. The figure was bound in a cord that was clearly magical. Not just spell-touched rope or whatever, the binds themselves were nothing but eldritch power. They weren't glowing, it was more like they were pulling all the light inside of themselves. What little light there was inside my nighttime bedroom.

It wasn't comfortable to look at, those bindings. I could just imagine how it must feel to have them touching your skin. Like they would suck in the heat from your body the same way they ate up all the light.

I shivered at the thought.

Then the bound figure tossed back a shimmering curtain of inky black hair and what light there was from the moon behind me hit the pale skin of her face.

My mother. It was my mother. Serena Greene. Bound up and seemingly helpless at my brother's feet.

"Houdini," I said. Or started to.

I'm not sure what I was going to say next. That he should go for help? That he should get us both out of there, back to the Tower?

Maybe that indecision was to blame. Maybe that provided the split second that was all my brother needed.

Or maybe, because he'd clearly been waiting for us, he was just that prepared.

Either way, I reacted too late. I realized the window that was supposed to be between us was not just standing open but entirely gone from its frame, too late. I realized my brother's hands were emerging from the darkness of my bedroom, too late.

I did flinch out of his grasp.

But it didn't matter. He wasn't trying to grab me. He was trying to grab Houdini.

And before my stupid brain even knew what was happening, he had him. My brother was clutching Houdini.

And then Houdini was gone. I couldn't see him inside the darkened room. And I couldn't hear his voice inside my mind.

He was just gone.

"Hush!" Mercutio hissed at me, grabbing my arm to drag me in through the window frame. He gave me a hard shake, and only then did I totally understand that I had been screaming out all my grief and rage. "He's just inside a pocket dimension. Safe and sound. I'll return him to you as soon as we're done here. I just can't have him doing... whatever it was he did last time."

I almost wanted to laugh at that. A crazy hysterical laughter was right on deck, bubbling at the back of my throat.

My stupid brother. He *still* didn't know what Houdini really was. And he had felt dragon breath blowing back his hair the last time he had threatened me. And felt the immensity of Houdini's dragon body standing protectively between us.

And he still thought Houdini was just an illicit familiar? Loyal servant to a broken witch?

But I didn't laugh. I just lunged for the light switch.

And almost laughed anyway when everyone else in the room flinched like a pair of Nosferatus in the paltry glare of my flickering overhead light bulb.

I was right about those bindings. They really did drink up the light. But their range was only a matter of inches. The rest of the room maintained its artificial glow.

Not that it helped me any. I could see no sign of where my brother had stowed the magical pocket he had stuffed Houdini into. Was it one of the pockets on his clothes?

But the tight black leather-like pants he was wearing didn't appear to have any pockets. The sheer white silk shirt he wore above it definitely didn't.

"I need you to listen," he said to me. He was holding his hands out in a pleading gesture, but I couldn't help noting that they, too, appeared to be empty.

"Where's Houdini?" I demanded.

"I told you, he's perfectly safe," Mercutio said. "You can trust me, Tabitha."

I snorted at that. Then I pondered leaping out of my window. From the veranda off my uncles' living room, I had a clear path to flee all the way down to the ground level of the Square.

But it was more than a ten-foot drop from my window to that veranda. And while I had many fine qualities, being athletic had never been one of them.

And my brother was standing between me and the only door out of my room.

I could try screaming again?

"Please," Mercutio said, as if reading my thoughts. "I went to all the trouble of bringing our mother here. We have to do this. We have to talk this out."

"What can she possibly have to say?" I demanded.

It was hard to think. My whole brain just kept saying Houdini-Houdini-Houdini over and over again in a loop.

"Well, that's why I brought her here, isn't it?" Mercutio said with dripping sarcasm. "If I knew what she was going to say without hearing her say it, I wouldn't have had to bother at all, would I?"

"You didn't already talk to her yourself?" I asked.

"I was waiting for the three of us to do this together," he said. "Tabitha, it's like you never listen to me at all."

"Ditto," I spat back at him.

But our mother was moving around now, not so much trying to free herself from her magical bonds as trying to get our attention. I realized there was another loop of that binding spell that stretched over her mouth, keeping her from even attempting muffled speech.

"Let her talk, then," I said. Although I made no attempt at looking like I was giving in with good grace. No, I was holding all the grudges. And there would be payback later.

But for now, I had to admit I was a little curious what she had to say for herself. I mean, we'd had so few conversations where I wasn't under the influence of her soporific magic. So few conversations I knew for a fact were real and not dreams.

It was almost like my mother was more a figment of my imagination than a flesh and blood woman.

And yet, here she was. In the glow of my bedroom light. Such as it was.

Mercutio mumbled something that sounded like maybe Latin, if badly pronounced. But it was close enough for the magical binding to respond to his command, letting the loop over our mother's mouth slip away.

"Tabitha! Mercutio!" she gasped the instant after she'd drawn in a full breath. "It's not safe for you here. You need to run. You've undone everything I've ever tried to do for you, both of you. But that doesn't matter now. You have to run!"

"Well, we can start there," Mercutio said as he settled himself on the foot of my bed. Like he expected this conversation was going to take a long time.

But the panic in my mother's eyes was getting to me.

I mean, the last time we'd been in this room together, she'd tried to take every last bit of my power away. I wasn't forgetting that. No, I was nicely nursing that anger for all it was worth.

But she was clearly very frightened, frightened out of her wits.

And for someone of her magical power to be this scared, whatever she was fearing had to be dangerous indeed.

"Is it our father?" I asked. I didn't sit down like my brother, but I did shift my weight to a more comfortable position, folding my arms and leaning a shoulder against the empty window frame behind me.

"Your father?" Serena repeated, as if she needed to say the words aloud to remember what they even meant. "No, your father is fine."

"Is he?" Mercutio asked. "This last month has been one revelation after another. Not only have I learned all sorts of things about the Ward family you never bothered to tell me, I also learned everything you *had* told me was basically lies. Lies. All lies." He stopped to seethe in a deep breath through his clenched teeth, then pulled himself together to say. "Whatever our father is, I wouldn't describe it as 'fine'."

Our mother just stared up at him as if he were deranged.

But then, as if she had heard or maybe just sensed something we had not, she started struggling against the magical bonds in real earnest.

"Stop that," Mercutio said, half getting up from the bed with something like genuine concern on his face. Then he remembered he was annoyed with our mother and sat back down without helping her. "They'll keep tightening the more you fight them. I suggest you stop before it gets too uncomfortable."

Then a horrible thought popped into my mind, and I pushed away from the wall. "Mercutio, please tell me this isn't faerie magic."

"What faerie magic responds to Latin?" he said to me with a snort.

"Binding is such a faerie thing," I said.

"It's not faerie magic," he snapped at me. "I'm not a complete fool."

"Aren't you?" our mother said coldly. "You're certainly choosing the fool's path right now."

"What do you mean?" I asked.

My mother looked up at me, but the pleading in her blue eyes was drowned out by that ever-present panic. "It's too late. Don't bother letting me go. I couldn't buy you any time now, even if I wanted to. I've bought you twenty-six years of time, but it's all gone now. It should've been more, but you both squandered it. Both of you!"

"What's she talking about?" Mercutio asked me.

I gaped at him. As if I knew a thing more than he did about anything. He had been the one living with her his entire life. I had been the secret, the one kept outside of everything.

"Run!" our mother roared at us both.

There was a magical oomph to that voice. I kind of felt the command spell she was trying to throw our way.

But it didn't really take hold. Maybe it was the bindings. Or maybe it was the influence of the bookshop extending even up into the attic, always looking out for me. But the urge to flee was like an itch on the bottom of my feet, easily ignored.

Then she just slumped again, letting the straight waves of her hair drape all around her to spill in puddles on the floor. I could no longer see her face, but the droop of her shoulders told me everything.

She was absolutely defeated. And the threat wasn't even here yet.

Then I heard footsteps coming up the stairs. A pair of them. Too light for my uncles.

Too many of them for my father. He had no minions that I knew of.

So who was coming up to my room?

"It's too late," my mother moaned into her own knees. "I did all I could. All I could for so long. But it's too late now."

I traded a confused glance with my brother. Then he got up from the bed to face the door. He shifted his weight into what was unmistakably a fighting stance.

For one perverse second, my only thought was the smug one that I had been right. My brother *did* study martial arts.

Then the door to my bedroom slammed open, and all my smugness was gone.

CHAPTER

SIXTEEN

I think, despite the fact I knew there had been two people coming up the stairs and that my father had no friends or minions or anything like it, that I was still expecting to see my father when that door blasted open.

Maybe he had conjured an elemental being to come with him. I don't know. There were possibilities.

I do know the last thing I had expected to see was Cleopatra Manx standing in my bedroom doorway in all her golden Inanna-aspiring beauty.

She was wearing a black minidress, as if for somewhat impractical but oh so fashionable night ops. Perhaps it was constructed of some tactical material, although there was no way it had any pockets in it. Not with the way it skimmed over her curves.

She *had* traded her usual entirely impractical footwear for ankle boots. But she still towered on top of the almost unmanageably tall heels of those boots.

Behind her, nearly lost behind the cloud of her perfectly blown-out golden hair, was a man I didn't know. And at first blush, he didn't look much like her. His dark brown hair was cut short on the sides but tall on the top in something between spikes and waves. Like he was growing out one look in favor of another but wasn't there yet.

But even past the sneer he was sending my way, I could see the fine bone structure of his face. And the color of his eyes. He was definitely Cleopatra's brother, a man I knew by name only.

Octavio Manx.

His name had turned up on our list of suspects on two different cases. In both, he had turned out not to be the culprit long before I had ever gotten around to trying to track him down.

Which would've been tricky. As the oldest son of one of the wealthiest, most powerful magical families, there would've been real barriers to getting an interview with him.

Not the least of which was his lifestyle. He was a socialite of sorts, according to his reputation. But the sorts of parties and functions he frequented were the sorts of dark, arcane gatherings that even other witches and magicians only spoke about in whispers.

And only when they absolutely had to.

So, all in all, not a pair of siblings I would have expected to find knocking on my bedroom door.

Although I wasn't exactly surprised when my brother Mercutio and Octavio Manx exchanged curt nods of mutual recognition.

Because, of course they knew each other.

"I told you she'd be here," Cleopatra tossed over her shoulder to her brother.

I was about to say something witty about it being my bedroom and all, when I realized they were talking about my mother.

Who was still bound on the floor. Bent over as she was, I doubted they realized her mouth was free.

But I also kind of doubted that gave her any kind of advantage.

Cleopatra stepped into the room without waiting to be invited in, looking around at my scattered things with a wrinkle of her nose in disgust that was basically an automatic response from her.

Her brother stayed in the doorway, watchful. He was also dressed all in black, but his pants, vest, and even the sleeves of his shirt were all bulging with pockets. He probably had most of the contents of a decent-sized hunting and fishing store in those pockets. I saw the butt of a knife in a sheath at his hip for sure, and another, smaller pair stuffed down the sides of his boots.

Knives. Weird choice for what was bound to be a magic fight.

Not that I was any better prepared.

"Where's Houdini?" I hissed at my brother.

He gaped at me as if that were the single stupidest thing I'd ever said.

"Thank you for bringing her here, Mercutio," Cleopatra purred as she stopped with her toes right in front of my mother's knees then squatted as low as she could get on those towering heels. She clearly wanted my mother to look up at her. But my mother was not cooperating.

"I didn't bring her for you," Mercutio said, then sent a new look my way, one of naked pleading.

"Relax," I told him. "Clearly, whatever you set in motion has spun outside of your control. I might believe she manipulated you, but I don't think she trusts you enough to be working with you."

"Always the astute observer, Tabitha Greene," Cleopatra said. But she wasn't looking at me. She was brushing her hands into my mother's hair to lift it away from her face.

Even now, Cleopatra couldn't hide the fact that she was a beautician by profession. Her gesture was just so practiced, sweeping the hair back then fastening it there with a clip I had no idea where she had gotten. It wasn't mine. She must've summoned it out of thin air.

Just to look at my mother's face.

My mother finally complied, lifting her chin to fix the full force of the glare from her icy blue eyes on the younger woman. Most people, even magical people, would've been rocked back by the venom in that gaze. Even I, on the periphery and not at all the target of that blast, felt myself taking half a step back.

But Cleopatra just smiled at her.

"You haven't won here," my mother said to her. "This isn't going to end how you think."

"Probably not," Cleopatra said with a careless shrug. "We've found the most success so far by carrying on without planning. So it pretty much has to end in a way that isn't what we think. Wouldn't you say, Octavio?"

Octavio just deepened his sneer but didn't leave my doorway.

Cleopatra shrugged again, this time at her brother. Then she straightened up out of her squat to tower over my mother.

"People have been looking for you," I said.

"I'm sure they have," Cleopatra said, as if she weren't really listening to me. She seemed to be mulling something over, but I didn't like the way her eyes kept dropping back down to my mother's once more bent head.

"Prosaic people," I said. "What's that all about?"

"Zoning laws," Cleopatra said.

It took me a second to realize she was being completely serious.

"What?" I said.

"Prosaic zoning laws," she said. "That man—Wendell Gorman, right?—was running for city council. He's also a property developer, looking to transform most of this neighborhood into chain stores and condos. You can imagine, once he started digging into things, how deeply confusing he found any prosaic records relating to our Square. Very confusing indeed."

"He's not supposed to notice," I said. "Even if he looks. Was he a sensitive?"

"Maybe," Cleopatra said brightly, as if she hadn't considered that idea before and found she liked it. "But, alas, not enough to be truly useful. I had to prod him to look again, over and over. He was an exhausting amount of work."

"I blame Cressida Cade," Octavio said. The first words he had spoken. I found I didn't like his voice, at all. It was like someone was grinding glass. It promised needless violence.

"What did Cressida do?" I asked.

"She was just a distraction," Cleopatra said with a dismissive wave of her hand. "A persistent distraction, perhaps. But nothing more than that."

"We should've killed her like you promised me we were going to," Octavio growled. "You've gotten too soft, living here. I told you. This place feasted on the entirety of your dark heart."

"Ew," Mercutio breathed out in disgust.

We all ignored him.

"I never spent a night here," Cleopatra said with another wave of her hand. Like she could dispel her brother's misgivings so easily. She clearly couldn't. He was still scowling as fiercely as ever.

"Why were you going to kill Cressida?" I asked.

"You never stop investigating, do you?" Cleopatra said with a laugh. "No? Well, that's fine. If you must know, we needed a body. Just a little dead someone to toss at your father's doorstep."

"To frame him for a murder? Lucentio Stanley tried and failed to do that just a month ago," I said.

"I think I'm a little more capable than an order mage driven mad by the loss of his chaotic sister," Cleopatra sniffed.

"Still. Maybe get a new idea?" I said.

"Listen, you—" Octavio said, taking half a step into the room.

But Cleopatra stopped his words and motion both with a single raised hand.

Then she smiled at me, that perfect magazine model smile that conveyed no warmth whatsoever, "Tabitha. It's sweet you're trying to protect your dad. And your mom here. But they're very bad people."

"That's not news," I said. "And what's the point of framing people who've already broken magical law? Why not just let them face justice for what they've actually done?"

"Please. They're too good at covering all that up," Cleopatra said. "Like your mother here. Your mother is an actual savant at cover-ups. Isn't that true, Serena, darling?"

My mother said nothing. She didn't even look up from the floor.

Although I did notice that, even bound up as she was, she had somehow gotten that clip back out of her hair. It all hung loosely around her in sheets again.

"Do you even know what your mother has been doing?" Cleopatra asked me with the clear air of a challenge.

"Of course I know what she's been doing," I said flatly.

I mean, I knew the parts of it that involved sucking out my power and leaving me a useless shell for most of my life. And I wasn't sure I cared about anything beyond that.

But Cleopatra just lifted one corner of her perfect mouth in a sneer. "No, I don't think you do. If you did, if you really did, she wouldn't be tied up here right now. And your whole attitude would be very, very different."

I couldn't help it. I looked at Mercutio to see if he had any idea what Cleopatra was hinting at. But he looked as confused as I felt.

He might not have been wrong about the need for the three of us to have a conversation face-to-face.

But Cleopatra caught that look and chuckled.

"No, you don't have a clue, either of you," she said. "But you will. The time is nearly here."

She looked pensive again, like she was calculating what to do next in her head.

I had no idea what was going on, but I knew any wrench I could throw into Cleopatra's mental works was a wrench I just had to throw.

"You wanted to frame my father. Why? To get him out of the Square?" I asked.

"Hm?" she said. But I had clearly interrupted her train of thought. "Oh, perhaps. Mainly it was a petty revenge thing, you know? I helped him get in here in the first place, and he was nowhere near as grateful as he ought to have been."

"My name is on the lease," Mercutio said suddenly. Like the thought had struck his mind and burst out of his mouth in the same instant.

"That's true," Cleopatra said with an indulgent grin. "It was supposed to be mine. He thought he was outwitting me there. There aren't very many of us magical types who even exist on paper in the outside world, and your mother went to great lengths to make sure you were one of them. As am I, for what it's worth. But it won't matter in the end. He can't save this place."

"My father was trying to save the Square?" I asked. Or, rather, kind of choked it out.

But Cleopatra just turned that condescending grin my way. "Oh, not for the sake of any of you people. Seriously. As if the Square were here to protect any of you or your precious neighborhood community. I'll be screaming with laughter when this place goes up in smoke, I promise you. I might keep the Tower, though. It needs a remodel, but the bones are good, as the prosaics say. I could love life inside my own ivory tower."

I was still processing all that when my mother lifted her head again. But this time it was me she was fixing with those icy blue eyes. Not in anger, or panic, or anything I'd ever seen before.

I kind of wanted to call it despair? But that still implied an emotional state. And honestly, I think my mother was past all of those.

"I did everything I could," she told me, her voice so hoarse you would think she'd been screaming for a solid hour instead of mostly being bound up and gagged. "I did everything I could to keep you from being used as pawns, but it's all over now."

"Yes, it's all over," Cleopatra said, even as she grabbed the binding across the back of my mother's shoulders and hauled her to her feet. "Nothing left but the endgame, right, darling? And we all know where we're going for that. Octavio, cuff the himbo."

Mercutio blinked as if he wasn't sure if that meant him or not.

"What about her?" Octavio asked, even as he fished a pair of magical manacles out of one of his many pockets.

"What, Tabitha Greene?" Cleopatra said with a jangling laugh. "Look at her hair, dear. So droopy. She's in no danger of setting anything on fire in the sad state she's in now. And short of that, she's not worth bothering with. Let her trot along after us if she likes. Or summon her failed friend or her prosaic pet. Her precious boyfriend is thoroughly tied up by now, thanks to her father. No, there's not a single thing she can do to stop us now."

Octavio somehow managed to laugh in my face even as he was cuffing my brother. Then he forced him out the door.

Cleopatra followed after, with my mother walking like a zombie in front of her.

"Steph," I said the minute I was alone.

"Steph," I said again, out loud and inside my head. I even dialed him on my phone.

"Stephanos Underwood!" I bellowed.

If it hadn't been the end of October, I probably would've heard crickets.

I bit my lip. I took out my phone and sent a quick text to the group thread that included Audrey and Liam as well as Steph.

Then I ran down the stairs. Kind of knowing that Cleopatra was absolutely right.

I didn't know what was happening. But I knew I didn't stand much chance of stopping it.

Still, I had to try.

SEVENTEEN

There was no sign of my uncles, and their apartment was dark save for the bedroom light that fell down the stairs behind me. The doors out to the veranda were all standing open, letting the wind swirl into the living room. Dried leaves were already accumulating on the sofa and in the corners by the bookshelves.

I raced out onto the veranda. I had only paused for a moment to try to reach Steph. The text I had sent had been only two words: hedge help. Not even any punctuation.

So where had the Manx siblings taken my mother and brother so fast?

I ran to the railing to look down and saw the two of them with upraised wands shining intensely, sparking with the creation of some powerful magic.

They still had my mother and brother bound between them. They were all descending on what appeared to be a ribbon of golden light. It curled and snapped through the air like the ribbons that gymnasts perform with, describing the end of an arc that was just taking them down to the nearest entrance to the hedge.

But the part of the arc where they must have started, up where I was standing at the veranda, was long gone now. It was a very truncated ribbon.

And I had no magic way of getting down after them. The best option besides taking the long way down staircase after staircase—not to mention jogging back and forth on the balconies the length of the Square—was the route I had mistakenly thought my brother had used to get up to me the other night.

Climbing down the dried vines of ivy, down all seven floors of the bookshop to the hard, unforgiving ground below.

It would mean a climb down the unadorned walls of the bookshop. If the ivy should start to give way, there'd be nothing else for me to hold on to. The brickwork was too neatly done. A champion climber could make do with those kinds of holds barely larger than a fingertip, but I would be sunk.

I threw a leg over the railing and grabbed great handfuls of vine, hoping for the best.

But I knew even if I fell the entire way down to the ground below, I'd still be moving too slowly to catch up with the others. They were already deep inside the maze.

I made it about halfway down from the edge of the veranda, still a frightful distance from the ground below, when I felt the vines start to pull away from their dried holds on the wall.

And without those anchor points, my weight started to tear the plant fibers themselves apart.

I tried moving faster, but that only seemed to make the whole disintegration of the vines happen faster as well. It was like they were turning to dust in my very hands.

And then my hands started to slip.

I yelped in alarm, just a single burst of involuntary sound.

But then that yelp morphed into a shriek of happy surprise. Because something was under me, holding me up.

Was it another snapping ribbon of gold? Or a fragment of one, maybe? Perhaps more of a flying carpet?

Whatever it was, it caught me like a cupped hand and carried me gently down to the grass below.

Where I saw my uncles waiting. My uncle Carlo had his wand out, a rare sight indeed. He seemed more discombobulated by the sight of it in his hand than I was, to judge from the near constant adjustments he was making to the frames of his glasses. But once I was safely on the ground, standing on my own two feet, he tucked that wand away again, and the golden light faded away.

And I saw I was standing on the faded rug from the area in front of the door of the bookshop. The one I had nearly set on fire when I had first come to the Square.

Before I could even ask what was going on, I was caught up in two massive bear hugs. Both of my uncles were crushing me at once, so tightly it was hard to breathe.

I wished I could stay there forever.

But there simply wasn't time.

"My mother," I gasped, and they both broke away from me.

"Serena is here?" Carlo asked. He reached up to touch his glasses again, but Frank stopped him, linking their arms together in a half-hug.

"She's inside the hedge maze," I said. "With Mercutio. Cleopatra Manx and her brother are up to something, and somehow it involves my mother."

"I'm guessing this is something we should be stopping," my uncle Carlo said grimly. "But we should hold here for a moment. The others are on their way."

"Others?" I said.

Even as Liam and Audrey came racing across the grass from the direction of, my first guess, her apartment.

But then I saw Cressida and Phoebe close behind them. Perhaps they were all coming from the salon, then. But why?

"We did it," Audrey told me as they all skidded, breathless, to a halt before my uncles and me.

"Did what?" I asked.

"The prosaic paperwork," Phoebe said. "Liam helped us. It's all in my name now. Cressida doesn't exist out there in the prosaic wold, but I do. And we're partners now in the magical world. So there is no attachment to Cleopatra anymore."

"That's great," I said, but I knew they could tell by my voice that I was pretty sure that was too little, too late.

"Tabitha," Liam said, coming closer to speak to me in a low voice. "Don't you remember? When I looked into the Square before I knew what it was, there was no record at all. How are there records now? We changed the name, but it doesn't feel like it's even going to matter."

"I think you're right," I said, glancing at my uncles to make sure they were listening too. "The protections are coming apart. The records being findable by prosaics is part of it. And Cleopatra absolutely made that happen. She was using this Wendell Gorman to poke at things she couldn't get at. Prosaic things. And I think it worked."

"They can see us now?" Cressida asked, glancing up at the walls of the bookshop towering over us.

"I'm not sure," I said. "The Wizard and Steph were about to do more reinforcing magic before I left the Tower, so maybe they're already on top of it."

Only I didn't know for sure. Because Steph hadn't answered my call.

"Or maybe this is finally what the Square has been preparing for," Audrey said grimly. "This moment, whatever is happening now. The Square wants us to run away."

"I have no intention of doing that," Cressida said, and Phoebe swallowed hard, but nodded her agreement with that remark.

"I don't want to either," Audrey said. She looked like she wanted to say something else, but my uncle interrupted her. He had something like wonder in his voice, an odd emotion in that particular moment.

"I think those aren't the only spells she's breaking apart," my uncle Carlo said.

"What do you mean?" I asked.

But even as the words came out of my mouth, I knew what he meant. I could see it in his eyes.

He remembered. He remembered all the things he could only remember before when I was holding his hand and letting the magic pendant that the Wizard and Steph had made for me extend its power to him. The pendant that kept me from the notice of powerful wizards like my father also let my uncle slip the bonds of his magical oath, if only for a moment.

But now, he was remembering all on his own. I wasn't touching him. I wasn't even particularly close to him.

"But wait," I said, confused. "That was a Ward family spell."

"I know," he said, taking off his glasses to wipe tears from the corners of his eyes. Then he settled them back on his nose and gave me a grim look. "What is happening here and now is only part of what the Manx family is doing. It extends so far beyond this. Whatever this is."

"The Wizard and Steph told me the dark magic families were allying against each other. Or picking sides in some coming secret war," I said, remembering. "That must be what this is. The Manx family making a power play to take out the Wards."

"Whomever your uncle swore his oath to, if the spell no longer holds him, that wizard must be dead," Audrey said.

"My great-grandfather, I guess," I said. "Maybe my grandfather too."

Which felt weird. I had never met them. They had barely reached out to my brother beyond ensuring that he bore their name.

And now I never would.

"Whatever they want with Serena," Carlo said, "We can't let them get it."

"So you don't know—?" I started to ask.

But he just shook his head, then caught my elbow to pull me

with him, intending for us both to head into the darkness of the hedge maze.

"Wait," Cressida said. She had been talking in intent whispers with Phoebe the entire time, but now they were looking not so much at me as at Audrey.

"We need to awaken all the shop spirits," Phoebe said without preamble.

"All of them?" I asked.

"All of them?" Audrey echoed, sounding already weary to the bone.

"All of them," Cressida said firmly. "Every shop. It might be the one thing that holds all this together." She put a hand in the air, gesturing vaguely to encompass the entire Square.

"I don't know—" I started to say.

But Audrey interrupted me. "I think they're right," she said. "I mean, I was about to suggest it before. As an alternative to abandoning the Square. Honestly, I don't know if I can even pull it off. But I'll do all I can."

"What good—" I started again.

But again she interrupted me. "Cleopatra doesn't know anything about *this* spell. She knew how to take down the spells that anchor us to prosaic bureaucracy. And who knows what else she's figured out. She's been a part of the Square for a very long time. She's had ample opportunity to study the structural magic and protective spells. And she's also been smarter than she gets credit for."

"She got Wendell Gorman inside without setting off any of the protections," I said. "I still don't know how that happened."

"Right," Audrey said. "But she won't have figured this out. Because she doesn't even know it's a thing. Steph and the Wizard don't have anything to do with it. And certainly none of the older wizards who created this place ever did anything like this. It's not anything she'll see coming."

I couldn't argue with any of that logic.

But I knew the look I gave her was one of regret at how much was being asked of her.

Although I couldn't even articulate why any of this felt at all like my fault. Like maybe I should've figured it out sooner, and stopped Cleopatra and her brother before they even got started.

Not that I had it figured out yet.

"I can do this," Audrey said, squeezing my elbow. "You just go and stop whatever they're doing with your mother."

"Mercutio put Houdini in a pocket dimension," I said, the words thick in my throat. "And Octavio Manx has my brother in magical manacles now. I don't know how I'm going to get him free."

"I do," Liam said.

We all gaped at him. Even Frank, who was also a prosaic. We were about to plunge ourselves into a magical combat that none of us had ever trained for. Liam and Frank, as prosaics, were clearly in way over their heads.

If there was a safe place I could send them to, I'd already be telling them to flee. But even with all the emergency exits extending out of the Square, it still felt like safety was so much further away than merely reaching the prosaic world.

But Liam just tightened his jaw and lifted his chin. "I can get close to Mercutio and find that pocket. These old magical families look down on prosaics, right? They think we're beneath notice. Not really fully human."

"Some of them," Carlo said.

"Then in that case, I'll be the closest thing to invisible," he said. "And Mercutio knows me, and so does Houdini. So they'll trust me, and help me get away afterwards."

"It's going to be dangerous," I said.

"I know," he said. "But it's getting more dangerous every second we delay."

"Time to run, then," I said.

I gave Audrey one last hug, hoping it conveyed all the strength I wished I could just magically hand over to her. Then I headed through the twisting archway of the hedge maze.

Carlo and Frank exchanged a long look. Then, hand in hand, they plunged in after me.

Liam lingered the longest to give Audrey a kiss goodbye. But then he jogged to catch up.

I saw Audrey standing with Cressida and Phoebe, watching us all leaving.

Then I took a turn that put the archway out of my view, and there was nothing around me but the rasping branches of autumn-dry hedges around me and the stars and harvest moon overhead.

But another light was glowing from where I knew the heart of the maze lay hidden. Something was happening with the portal.

"Is that on schedule?" Frank asked, even as I wondered the same thing.

"Don't think so," Carlo answered, already halfway out of breath from jogging. It was a shame we couldn't use a magical carpet or flying ribbon or some other contrivance to get us directly there, but the maze wouldn't allow it.

We had to navigate the labyrinth to get to the heart of things. And as much as I had long ago memorized every twist and turn, it was still a circuitous route.

But the light grew brighter with every turn. Whatever was happening with the portal, it was putting out silvery light brighter by far than the orange moon above.

I burst into a sprint when I knew I was getting close to the end, banking tightly around the last few corners.

Then I was in the heart of the maze, right where we had found the body of Wendell Gorman.

My mother was there, slumped on the ground almost exactly where Cressida had been that fateful night.

My brother was at the periphery of the space, only the light reflecting off of his sheer white shirt giving his presence away. Octavio Manx was still beside him, wand raised menacingly.

But he wasn't menacing my brother with that wand.

He wasn't directing it at my mother, either. Cleopatra had her covered well enough. Although she, with wand drawn, was paying no more attention to Serena than Octavio was to Mercutio.

No, every eye in the place, even my mother's from under the dark sheets of her hair, was directed at the other opening into the hedge maze. The one that came in from the north.

And I saw the Wizard and Steph standing there, hands out in a way that told me they had just teleported in and were still getting their bearings.

A process that would only take them a split second to accomplish.

But even as I watched them recover, I saw another flash between them. And my father was there too.

"Serena," he said, and pulled the green-tinted lenses from his eyes to look at her more directly.

"Benvolio," she said in a seething huff.

"You've done your best, dear. But the time has come to be gracious in defeat. Wouldn't you say?" he purred at her.

She looked down at the bonds holding her arms tight to her sides, then back up at him, but said nothing.

"I do hope you're ready," he said. His hand made a motion, flipping back the folds of his coat. Like he was reaching for a wand.

My mother lifted her chin a little, as if to be sure he saw the gleam of her teeth as she grinned maniacally at him.

The Manxs had seen none of this, both of them standing behind my mother's back. But whatever was about to happen, I knew it wasn't anything they had planned for.

Although I wasn't sure if that meant it was going to be anything even remotely good.

Then my father returned my mother's grin. His was just a quirk of the corner of his mouth, almost a sneer, and then I was sure.

I was very sure.

This wasn't going to be good.

CHAPTER

EIGHTEEN

Just as the Manxs couldn't see my mother's crazy grin, the Wizard and Steph couldn't see Benvolio's answering sneer.

Only I knew that something was passing between my parents.

Well, me and my uncles beside me, and Liam just behind us.

And for a second, it felt like everyone in that clearing around the ancient stone arch that marked the location of the portal was frozen in place. We were trapped in a tableau in the flickering silver light still spilling out intensely from between the broken stone pillars of that arch.

This light show wasn't what it looked like when the portal was opening to let magical types come and go from all the other portals around the world.

I didn't know *what* it was, but it definitely wasn't that.

Then Steph said, "Tabitha," breathlessly.

Just my name. But it was enough to break the spell. And not just on me.

Octavio Manx advanced closer to his sister, both of them still with wands high but clearly now aiming them directly at my father.

My mother was settling herself back on her feet. She was still kneeling, but her weight was resting on her heels now, as if she had just finished stretching out in child's pose.

Like she expected to be there for a bit, watching and waiting.

Liam behind me was already fading into the shadows against the hedges, creeping through as much darkness as he could find, creeping towards Mercutio.

Steph looked immensely relieved to see me. More than the bit of time we'd been apart should merit, but not as if he realized that I had been calling out for him without response. I wanted to ask where he had been and why he hadn't heard me.

But my uncle was the first one to speak. He, still hand in hand with Frank, stepped further into the light, towards the Wizard. "The spells that protect the Square are failing. The prosaics are growing aware of us."

"I know," the Wizard said with a tired nod. "We are working on it."

"It's more than that," I said. "Aside from violating the terms of her house arrest and kidnaping my mother and brother, Cleopatra Manx has also been making moves against the Ward family."

"Please. As if you even know what you're talking about," Cleopatra said with an exaggerated eye roll.

"You can hardly argue that you haven't done those things, not when you're standing here *not* in your family's home, and with my mother and brother currently bound in magic, unable to move," I said. I might have flailed a little, but everyone knew my emotions were running high.

That flailing certainly drew enough attention away for Octavio not to notice Liam sneaking closer to Mercutio's side behind him.

"The authorities should definitely be summoned," my father said, but with a sneering tone of irony to his voice.

He didn't pull out his wand. He just made a little flicking gesture with his hand.

And just like that, Cleopatra Manx was tied up in bindings of dark magic, including a loop that extended across her mouth.

And Octavio swore aloud as a spare set of his own manacles snapped closed over his wrists.

Although somehow I doubted my father had done anything to summon the sheriff. He would want to be long gone before arrests were made.

"Benvolio," my uncle Carlo said.

My father actually startled at the sound of my uncle's voice. Then he stopped in mid gesture whatever spell he had been about to cast next and turned to look at my uncle.

"Carlo Greene," he said. "You're not supposed to speak my name. You not supposed to even be able to."

"That's what my niece is trying to tell you," my uncle said. "The Manx family has done something. I'm free to speak. I have every memory back. I don't think either situation is going to change again anytime soon. I can feel it in my bones. The spell is broken. I've been released from my oath of silence."

My father half-closed his eyes, for all the world as if he were consulting his own bones.

When he opened them fully again, the scowling frown on his face was so dark it was like the magical binding around Cleopatra's and my mother's bodies, sucking in the light around it.

"My grandfather," he said. "And my father too?"

Cleopatra couldn't speak with that dark cord of magic over her mouth. She couldn't even laugh. But her eyes spoke volumes. Their laughter answered all my father's questions.

But Octavio clearly wanted things to be clearer than that. "They're both dead by now, old man!" he barked out, then cackled.

"How?" Benvolio asked, but without emotion. As if he merely needed the answer so he could complete some sort of form.

"The Unveiled Guild!" Octavio declared.

"They would never," my father said.

But he just looked at my uncle Carlo, who looked back at him with complete recognition. And obvious distaste.

Then my father closed his right hand into a tight fist. "We've waited too long," he said.

The Wizard and Steph exchanged a look, as if wondering if he was talking to them.

But I knew who he was talking to. He was talking to my mother.

"I tried to tell you," she said. "This was never going to work the way you wanted it to."

"How did *she* even find out?" my father suddenly bellowed, jabbing a finger at Cleopatra, then advancing closer to my mother with that fist at the ready.

But my mother only blinked up at him impassively.

"I never told her. I never told a soul," she said. "But she's been spending her days inside the Square for years now. She's not as blind and deluded as most here. It was only a matter of time before *someone* sensed it. Why not her? The Manx family has always been the chiefest rival to the Ward family. Their power just might be greater than yours."

"Nonsense," my father spat out.

Cleopatra might be bound and gagged, but her eyebrows were still capable of arching. She could project disdain like nobody's business.

But my father brushed past her without so much as a glance at her. Now he was standing directly over my mother.

"What does the rivalry between two families who aren't even based in this city have to do with the protections of our Square?" I demanded.

My mother glanced up at me, then just as quickly dismissed me from her mind.

My father never looked around at me at all.

But the Wizard stepped forward. "The question stands, Benvolio," he said. "You must answer it."

My soul ached, watching the old man moved. There was more

than exhaustion dogging his steps. I could feel the pain in his joints just watching him limp a few steps closer to the glowing portal.

"Oh, must I?" my father sneered.

"It's not about the Square," my mother said suddenly. "It's about the portal."

"What about the portal?" Steph asked. "It has power, sure. It connects us to other magical neighborhoods all around the world. It takes a tremendous outlay of power to keep that running. But it's just one node. One part of a much larger network. And if the Ward or Manx family wanted to control that network, this isn't where they'd go to start that takeover."

"It's not about the transportation network," my father spat out, as if that were the stupidest thought he'd heard in a great long while.

"I grew up here, you know," my mother said. Everyone was listening to her, but her eyes were only on me. And there was something almost human there now, a warmth that was at least a shadow of maternal feeling. "That room you sleep in, it was my bedroom when I was a girl."

"I didn't know you grew up in the bookshop," I said.

"Oh, it wasn't a bookshop then. Just a little general store," she said. "Your uncle grew that bookshop later. He put all of his power into it."

"That's a lot of power," Steph said.

"The Greenes don't like to compete with the grand old families," my uncle Carlo said with an adjustment to his glasses. "But that doesn't mean we couldn't. We have the magic. We just don't have the ambition. We're... recluses."

"We're recluses because we have to be," my mother said fiercely. "Generation after generation, almost all of us are either chaos mages or order mages. And so, generation after generation, we have to hide just what we can really do. We have to dump the magic wherever we can. That's not exactly easy, you know."

"Little worth doing comes easy. And you ended up with a collection of books that outdoes the All-Planes Athenaeum," the Wizard mused. "Not to mention my own personal collection. That is a tremendous outlay of order magic."

"Yes, but the problem is, my sister generated just as much chaos magic," my uncle Carlo said. "No, that's not even right, is it, sister?"

"*You* had to match *me*," she said. "Left to your own devices, you never would've channeled so much order magic. You'd have been quite content with a tiny little bookshop, just enough for you and your husband."

"How much chaos were you generating?" Steph asked.

"And where were you putting it, dear?" the Wizard asked.

His words were kind, but his tone had an edge to it. Because he had been protecting the Square since before my mother was born. Her girlhood in the Square, he had been there the entire time.

A chaos mage had been under his very nose since long before I had arrived in the Square.

And, I could tell by the look in his eyes, he had never had a clue. She had actually been generating chaos. She had been carrying chaos magic around. And the Wizard had never sensed it.

But my mother just laughed.

"You took my power too," I said. "My whole life, you've been taking my power, too. Where have you put it all?"

"In the portal," Steph said, because it was the only conclusion that made sense.

But we all looked at the portal among us. It was a powerful magical artifact, but it was very far from unique. Every major magical neighborhood the world round had one. The larger neighborhoods had more than one.

The Square's portal was a modest one.

And yet, just what was causing the silvery light that was dancing out of it now?

Because I had passed through that portal to get to other places, and that light had been all rainbows. This? This was something very different.

And yet, the silver light with its moon intensity, it reminded me so much of my mother. With her inky black hair and her pale skin. That silver light just felt like it was a part of her.

But surely chaos couldn't be so calmly pretty?

"You put it all inside the portal," I guessed. My mother said nothing. Neither did anyone else. But I found myself walking a few steps closer to that light, like it was drawing me in. "You found a way to open a doorway to somewhere else. Somewhere the portal isn't supposed to go. Some other dimension, maybe. And you put all your power and mine inside there, like you were storing it."

Her steady gaze gave me nothing, but I was sure I was right. Or, at least, I was getting close.

But I still didn't have an answer why.

"For my father's grand designs, I'm guessing?" I said. "Maybe not at first. It sounds like you just needed to discharge extra magic."

Like my mother had had a childhood a lot like mine. With random fires and school experiments going explosively sideways.

A childhood filled with dangerous levels of chaos.

I pushed the wave of empathy down hard like I was swallowing back bile and pressed on. "But after you met my dad, this was totally about his grand plan. At least at first. You parted ways before I was born. I guess you never really told him about this? But you kept using it. For my chaos and for your own. And just like you hid me, you needed a place to hide all that chaos away. And yet Cleopatra Manx found out about it. And she came here now to take it from you."

"She wanted to control the portal," my mother said. "But even if she had it in her possession, if the Manx family had owned all the Square and everything inside it, it wouldn't have made any difference. She is neither a chaos mage nor an order mage. There isn't a single thing she can do to access this power."

"She forced you to open this doorway," Steph said.

A guess, but from her scowl, an accurate one.

"I can turn it back at any time," she said. "I don't even need to be unbound to do it. It's my power."

"And mine," I said.

"But I control the doorway," she said. "I can hold all the chaos behind it forever if I want to."

"All Cleopatra can do is sit on it and keep it from you," Steph said.

"Well, she failed," my father said with a shrug. "And now it's all mine. And I'll be taking it now. I expect you'll try to stop me, Fortinbras. But I think we both know you're too weakened by our efforts earlier to hold the Square together to have any hope of succeeding. Still, please feel free to try."

He made another flick of his wrist, and my mother was suddenly unbound. Free.

But rather than running away, she got to her feet, turned to the portal, and reached out her arms.

I only had a split second to gape in shock. She was working with him? After everything that had happened since before I was ever born up until mere seconds before, she was still working with him?

Then it didn't matter. Because suddenly the entire world was sparking madness. That beautiful silver glow was now a riot of eldritch explosions.

We were all being showered in the hot shrapnel of pure chaos.

CHAPTER

NINETEEN

I knew the feeling of this magic. I had felt it before. It was chaos in its purest form. As much as my mother had spent her lifetime trying to deprive me of this feeling, I knew it still. I had only known it in snatches before, but it washed over me now in wave after wave of exultant familiarity.

But I could hear everyone around me screaming. Screaming in pain, in fear, in helpless despair.

Even the Wizard.

This feeling I knew so well was beyond even him.

I had spent my whole life trying to find little ways to be helpful. Without magic of my own—or so I had thought at the time—I found other things to be good at.

Writing spells I couldn't perform myself. Researching books on magic I could never even hope to attempt.

But this? This pure, raw chaos? This might very well be what I was born for.

I opened my eyes wide despite the dazzling intensity of the power that was bathing the entire heart of the hedge maze. The hedges were on fire, a crackling building up to a roar as the dry leaves caught.

My friends were rolling on the dried grass, trying to put out the flames that were consuming their clothing. Mostly, they were just igniting the grass.

But there was nothing I could do to help them. So I forced myself to look away from them and towards the portal. To see what was really going on.

My mother was there, right between the two stone pillars, standing with her arms wide. But she wasn't bathing in that power.

She was *adding* to it. Even as I watched, I saw her generating more and more chaos. Generating it, and feeding it into that silvery pool inside the portal. It was still so beautiful in there.

My father, on the other hand? He was drinking it in.

And that I just knew I had to stop.

I charged forward, getting between my parents and the portal they were using as a channel between her chaos magic and his order magic. I couldn't suck it all up. It was too much.

But I could do enough. I could buy the Wizard and Steph a little bit of time. They were summoning great quantities of water out of the cloudless sky to put out the flames, but I could hear the fire spreading.

The whole maze was going up like so much dried tinder.

"Protect the Square!" I bellowed to them both, even as the magic I was pulling into myself was making all my nerve endings tingle. It was a tingle that was building in intensity, and I knew even I would be burning soon. "Audrey and the others are conjuring protecting spirits, but you have to help the Square itself. You have to hold it together!"

"They *are* helping," Steph said to the Wizard, although it sounded like he was speaking through gritted teeth. "The spirits. I can feel them. We can use them."

The Wizard said nothing.

My father was glaring at me, but he didn't dare try to touch me.

Maybe I was a little bit on fire already, or maybe he just knew it wouldn't do any good. But he took a step closer to the portal and attempted to pull more of the magic from it before I could wick it away out of his reach.

My mother, on my other side, was weakening already. I didn't think she'd had much power left in her when the fight had started. She never let it accumulate in her own body any more than she'd ever let it accumulate in mine. It had all been going inside the portal.

We had both come into the hedge maze tonight thoroughly tapped out.

But as much as I could soak it up, I couldn't really channel that magic. I wasn't an order mage. And what I was trying to do was a lot like trying to put toothpaste back in the tube. I was the source, the creator. Things flowed out of me, not into me. I wasn't a battery. I couldn't hold in chaos that way. Pulling in more power, even if it was meant to be my own power, was going to burn me up.

I certainly knew that from experience.

I gritted my teeth and tried to power through the burning pain. I just needed to buy the Wizard and Steph more time. So they could save the Square.

"You can't do this!" my mother bellowed at me. She had stumbled over to my side and was attempting to grab my arm. But even she didn't dare touch me. Eldritch flames were licking all over me. Not fire, not yet, but certainly scary to look at. And kind of painful, if I'm being honest. "It's too much for you, Tabitha! It's not your power. Just let it go!"

"It's mine," my father said, taking another half a step closer to the portal. And, indeed, the power that was burning me up was flowing into him so naturally. He was acquiring a bit of a glow, but he was totally in control.

But I knew in my bones, the last thing I wanted was my father in control of all that magic.

What was his plan? To destroy everything and rebuild it to his own design? His own idea of what order was?

He said nothing, just drank in that power as he took another half a step closer to the source. But I could see it in his eyes.

That *was* his plan. He wanted a tower and freedom to study chaos and order as a wizard. But that was all for later.

First, he had to create a new world order, starting with the Square. But then spreading everywhere, to all magical neighborhoods all over the world.

And nothing the Manx family did was going to stop him. He didn't need the old Ward family anymore. They had disowned him anyway. He would establish a new Ward family, with himself as the patriarch.

I felt my uncle Carlo trying to move closer, trying to help out. But even as I sensed his approach, so did my father. Benvolio didn't even turn to confront my uncle. He just tossed another flick of his wrist, and my uncle went sailing through the air, crashing through the wet but still smoldering hedges somewhere in the darkness behind us.

I heard Frank call out Carlo's name and go charging after him, but still I didn't dare turn to look.

I took a step closer to the portal and redoubled my efforts to draw away the power before my father could have it.

He just sneered at me.

But then my brother was there beside me, standing shoulder to shoulder with me despite the flames dancing over my skin and singeing my clothes. He was drawing in the power too, faster than my father could. Like he was the emptiest of sponges and my father was already sopping, too full to drink up anymore with any speed.

"Hey," Mercutio said with a grin. "We should've been doing this forever, right? Moving magic between us?"

But I couldn't return his grin. "Where's Houdini?" I gritted out.

He gave me a puzzled frown. "You're worried about your dog *now*?"

"Serena, you really shouldn't have shut me out of our children's lives," my father said sardonically. "Do you see what they're doing?"

"Ruining everything?" my brother taunted him.

"As if you even could," my father said. "Serena?"

But she refused to match his jocular tone. She was angry again, angry and desperate. "Let them go," she said. "Let them go, or I won't help you at all."

"I'm not holding them here, darling," my father said. "Why don't you send them away so we can finish this together?"

She nodded glumly. Then she turned her attention to me.

"Tabitha," she started to say.

But I was having none of it. "No. Whatever you're doing here, you're sacrificing the Square to do it. And I won't allow that."

"You've been here for five months," my mother snapped at me. "Five months. That's a moment in time. It's nothing."

"It's everything," I said. I risked a glance over at the Wizard and Steph. They were gesturing with their wands, weaving elaborate layers of spells I could only guess at the purpose of.

Steph was bathed in sweat, his face pale and thin as if his body was burning off every calorie he'd ever consumed all in this one final effort.

The Wizard was half-stooped under the weight of his exhaustion now, but he wasn't stopping.

They were holding everything together, but I was afraid they were only just accomplishing that. The minute exhaustion took them, the spells would fail. Not even the shop spirits could hold everything together, not once the Wizard collapsed.

But there didn't seem to be any end to the magic streaming out of that portal.

Then Mercutio, by my side, said, "Um, Tabitha? I'm starting to feel a little funny."

I looked over at him and saw the eldritch flames that danced all over my body were now doing elaborate patterns all over his. Only, unlike me, he wasn't used to this. He had never been on fire before.

Our father sneered. "I've trained my entire life for this moment. What little you take won't matter. Your mother has poured a lifetime into this font. You two simply don't have the skill or the practice to be of any use here."

"We're not alone," I said, even as Mercutio stopped drawing the power. He was hissing in pain. I knew he was trying to control it, but he didn't stand much chance.

Like our father said, he had never trained in this.

And it wasn't exactly intuitive.

"Everyone in the Square is bolstering Steph and the Wizard now," I said.

And somehow I knew that was absolutely true. I mean, the idea that Audrey, Cressida and Phoebe, Titus and Violenta, and frankly everyone else in the Square would flee for safety was insane. They may not be inside the hedge maze with us, which, given the chaos shrapnel all around us, was for the best. But they were still fighting. They were holding the world together around us, I just knew it.

They were preserving the perfect order of our shared home.

"It won't make any difference," my father assured me. "Once all the magic is inside me, I'll be making all the rules. And you *will* be alone."

I couldn't help it. I flinched. Those words struck me to the core. Just like he had known they would.

But then another voice entered the conversation.

"Tabitha Greene will never be alone."

I recognized that voice at once. Of course I did. It was my constant companion, the warm tone that was the first thing I heard in my mind in the morning and the last thing I heard at night.

It was Houdini.

Liam had done it. He had found the pocket and released Houdini.

And he was speaking in everyone's minds now. I guess the time really had come. There were no secrets anymore, not inside the Square. Everyone would know now. He was no ordinary dog, despite all appearances.

Then he was standing in front of me, facing my father. Although he wasn't growling, the hair was bristled in a ridge all the way up his back.

And it was like I could see Houdini growing. He was still a little dog, but I was aware of his dragon form, too. Like when he had chased Mercutio away when my brother had attempted to release my power the month before, Houdini was letting everyone feel his full size.

It was far bigger than three elephants now. It had to be ten, or more.

My father—who had only this evening ever kicked his sneer up or down a few notches without ever quite losing it—looked downright terrified now. I could see the breath from the unseen dragon nostrils blowing his hair back.

Blowing it back from above—far above—his head.

And he faltered in drawing in the power. Just a flicker, but I knew he was about to fall back. Maybe just for a moment, but it would be enough.

Mercutio, beside me, was already dropping into a fighting stance, ready to charge in the minute there was any advantage to be pressed.

But then, seemingly out of nowhere, my mother rushed in. She bent down and scooped up Houdini.

It was like the dragon form didn't exist for her at all. All she held was a perfectly ordinary rat terrier chihuahua.

A shaking, terrified little dog. He looked to me in real alarm.

But before I could so much as move a muscle, he was gone. My mother had flung him into that portal.

Into that font of pure chaos.

And with a single startled yelp in the back of my mind, he was gone. He was out of this world.

And I truly was alone.

CHAPTER

TWENTY

For the longest six seconds of my life, my soul was torn in two. I just stood there in complete and total shock. It was like the two broken halves of my soul were too far apart to even begin to start grieving.

Or raging. In a way, I *was* raging. All the power I had been pulling in exploded out of me in a blast I only just managed to fire up into the sky and not toast my friends.

But I didn't feel that rage. I felt numb.

I was too broken to feel anything at all.

But even the longest six seconds of my life were still only six ticks of a clock.

Then a swirling pattern emerged from the heart of the silvery chaos. This was more like the portal in its working state, all rainbow colors and sparkling lights.

And yet, it was different. As if the rainbow I was looking at now contained more colors than my eyes could even perceive. My stunted magical senses were picking up so much more. But it was like trying to pick out words on a radio station that is mostly static. I couldn't quite get a handle on any of it. But I knew I was missing out on something.

Then the swirling pattern sped up into a typhoon. No, a whirlpool. I was looking at the surface, and the swirling cone was extending down into it, further and further away from me. Like a tunnel into something, although I couldn't see what lay beyond. The far end was all twisting darkness.

Six more seconds ticked by while I gazed in dazed awe at whatever was happening before me.

I kind of sensed my parents stumbling back from the stone archway in sudden panic. Then my brother, taking their cue, did the same.

But I was rooted to the spot. I couldn't take a step closer to that spinning madness, but I definitely couldn't take a step back.

Houdini was in there. Somewhere.

Then the twisting funnel started to writhe. It was like I was watching a snake swallowing a mouse, only in reverse.

Actually, it was a lot like that. It was about to puke something out at me. But before I could make another attempt at stepping back out of the way, something exploded out of that funnel, right into my arms.

"Houdini!"

"Tabitha!" he said, breathless even in the back of my mind.

"You've lost your collar," I said, although that seemed like a minimal point at that moment.

Only, really, it wasn't.

"You've lost your collar, but you're still a dog," I said.

Because all the spells that Agatha had done to protect Houdini from the notice of dragon-hunting mages had been worked into that little strip of leather. And if it was gone now, how were the spells holding?

"I have so much to tell you," he enthused.

"You were gone for like twenty seconds," I said.

Twenty-four, actually, but who was counting?

"Oh, yes. They told me they couldn't get me quite back to where I was, but they did say it would be very close," he said.

"Who said?" I asked. The first of about a thousand questions.

But Houdini barely got out the words, "My parents," before the funnel behind him started to writhe around again.

And this time, I really did think I ought to step back.

Like, way, way back.

Holding Houdini close against my chest, I ran backwards until I reached the charred branches of the remains of the hedge. Somehow, in all the arguing and fighting and channeling of magic, my inner navigator had gotten turned all around. I didn't know quite where the doorway was back out of the heart of the maze.

But I saw my uncles just on my right, and Liam covered in soot for reasons I didn't even want to imagine a little farther away on my left. Maybe we were all trapped.

There was a burst of light, like an atomic bomb going off, and it took a long time before I could blink my eyes back into clear vision.

But when I did, I saw the portal between the stone pillars of the broken archway had gone dormant. It looked as empty as I felt. There was no silver light or rainbow tunnel or anything, just an ordinary view of the charred remains of the hedge on the far side.

The whole hedge maze must have burned mostly to the ground. I knew the Wizard and Steph had been dumping water on it from above. I knew they had put out the flames.

But I hadn't realized that it hadn't mattered. It hadn't been in time. The hedge was nothing but smoldering stumps and charred branches that were raining down in clouds of ash at the slightest touch of a breeze.

I didn't quite have time to take all that in, though, before I noticed what was standing between me and that view through the archway.

I could be forgiven for not noticing at once. The magic around them was even stronger than the magic around the Tower. My gaze just kept wanting to slip past them. And even when I realized something was there and tried to focus my attention on it, it was like looking at slippery ghostly forms.

But there was no question what those ghostly forms were of.

They were dragons. Two immense dragons. They filled the entire center of the hedge maze. It was a good thing all of us humans had already fallen back against the remains of the hedges, because there wouldn't have been room for any of us when these two emerged from that tunnel.

Although I wasn't sure if they would actually have crushed anything. They were standing on the singed and now frost-covered grass, but their massive feet weren't leaving any kind of mark on that ground. I could see a few rare stalks of grass still jutting up into the air, uncrushed by what had to be the weight of hundreds of elephants.

And yet, the longer I focused on looking at them, the more details I could take in. Their ghost qualities gave them a silvery glow, but beyond that, their scales had a rainbow sheen. Like they were made of living quartz, they had the kind of opalescence where every change in the light brings a newer, deeper beauty.

I could also kind of tell that the larger one was Houdini's mother, and the smaller, lither one his father. It was just something about their faces. Or, perhaps, it was the way that the long, whiskery feelers that framed the smaller one's face put me in mind of the sort of long mustaches that a sage would grow so he could stroke them while pondering the universe.

"Greetings," the Wizard said. His voice rang out so brightly through the cold, quiet night air that we all involuntarily flinched a bit. At the sound of it, my spirits lifted, because he sounded as spry as he ever did on his best days.

But then I saw him, dangling limply in Steph's weary embrace, and I knew they were both just as beyond exhausted by their efforts as I had thought they were.

If these dragons came for a fight, it was going to be a brief one.

But no. These were Houdini's *parents*. Surely they hadn't come looking for a fight?

Houdini was squirming in my arms, and I bent to set him down on the ground. He charged over to the dragons, up on his hind legs long before his front paws could touch anything. He jumped all around them, higher and higher, as if he wanted to be picked up.

Just like he did every time we were apart for more than a matter of minutes. He was living his puppy days all over again.

Then the mother dragon made a sound I couldn't understand or even work out phonetically. But I gathered this was her name for Houdini, as he quieted at once, even before she carried on with, "Behave yourself, dragonet. This is a diplomatic mission."

"Sorry," Houdini said sheepishly, although his tail was still wagging like mad. "It's this dog form. It comes with certain overwhelming urges. I think I forgot for a time how strong they were."

I frowned at those words. Just how long had he been away, on the other side of the portal? He looked the same, and yet he sounded different. More mature, maybe.

Like it had been years for him.

"I gather this dragonet here has told you all about what's happened here, at least from his perspective," the Wizard said. He leaned against Steph, trying to straighten a little taller, but he was barely staying on his feet, so it didn't help much.

Houdini's father gave him a measured look. "He has. We have also been watching through this rift, as has become our custom since we found it."

"We had debated closing it up again for some time," Houdini's mother said. "From the moment it was first formed."

"But curiosity is our greatest vice," the father dragon said.

"For which we've paid bitterly," the mother dragon said, and bent down to nudge Houdini's tiny form with her snout. By all rights, she should've knocked him flat even with the gentlest of touches. But she had far more control over her immense form than I would've imagined. Like a dancer.

Or perhaps more like one of those hobbyists that makes ridiculously small miniatures with pieces the size of grains of sand carefully placed with the finest of tweezers.

"Oh, I see," the Wizard said.

And so did I. The rift my mother had inadvertently created by dumping her chaos magic into the portal, the rift she had grown throughout her life and then mine by adding to that power, that rift was how Houdini had ended up in our world in the first place. His egg had been drawn to the safety of the Tower, but only after mistakenly rolling through the rift in the first place.

"Curiosity is our greatest vice," the father dragon said again. But this time fondly, as he gazed down at his son.

"He moved himself around while still inside the egg?" Steph asked.

"Telekinesis," the Wizard whispered to him. But loud enough for all of us to hear.

"I'm not any kind of dragon in any of your books," Houdini said proudly. "My parents are the rarest kind of dragons, and even if I spoke the name of their kind, you wouldn't understand it."

"It is a labor to be understood by you even so much as we are now," his father put in.

"We deeply appreciate the effort," the Wizard said. "And you speak marvelously well."

"Our son was truly an excellent teacher, then," Houdini's mother said, and gave him another soft nuzzle.

"We will have to mend this rift now, of course," his father went on. "We left it open too long as it is."

"Such things are forbidden for a reason," his mother said with a sigh. "Or so the others keep telling us."

"We're rather rebels, ourselves," his father said.

"I won't ask you to utter your name here, but may I take a guess as to the nature of your being?" the Wizard asked. The two dragons shared a long conferring gaze, then each nodded a considered assent. "Thank you. I believe what you might be is a sort of ur-dragon. The original branch before all the others evolved. That is how Houdini can channel the characteristics of every kind of dragon we've ever encountered on this plane. Because you contain them all?"

"An interesting theory," Houdini's father said after a long moment's thought.

"Our own origins aren't anything that interests us very much," his mother said.

"You're not curious?" I asked. I couldn't help the grin when I used that word.

"Not about ourselves," she said. "I suppose what we strive to understand is more ur-something else."

"Such as the substance of this rift you've created," Houdini's father said. "Chaos and order in such regimented flows. So strange for us. We've moved beyond such concepts so long ago."

"Our dragonet had to explain it to us again oh so many times before we grasped the nature of your problem," his mother said.

But now it was my father, pushing away from the burned remains of the hedge and drawing up his spine to stand tall, who spoke. "You understand the essences of chaos and order? You've studied it? It's forbidden here, but I am, as you call yourselves, curious. I would desperately love to learn all you have to teach on this matter."

The Wizard was looking from the dragons to Benvolio and back again with a worried frown. I could tell he was debating when he should interfere.

But he didn't have long before his inner debate became moot. Houdini's father rose up even taller than before and fixed my father with the darkest of stares.

"Then it is fortunate for you that we've already agreed to undertake your education," he roared.

His feet might not be making any indentation on the grass beneath him, but his voice was shaking the entire Square. I wouldn't be surprised if the prosaic world outside our magical neighborhood could even feel it. A surprise Minnesotan earthquake.

My father was looking immensely pleased with himself, smoothing down the front of his long black coat.

It was missing more than a few buttons now, I couldn't help noticing.

But now it was my mother's voice piping up from where she cowered in amidst the deepest patch of surviving hedge. "You're taking him away?" she asked in a wavering voice.

"Taking him away," I repeated, then looked at Houdini.

"It was my idea," he admitted, not even trying not to sound smug.

"You're taking him away to educate him?" the Wizard asked, bemused.

"You're starting to make it sound like they're going to incarcerate me," Benvolio said with a sly grin. "But this is everything I've ever wanted. Finally, I will know all there is to know about my power and how best to use it."

"I don't want to learn more about my power," my mother said. "I never did. I just want it gone. Can't you make it gone?"

"I'm sorry, Serena Greene," Houdini's mother said. Although not particularly apologetically. But then, if everything she knew about my mother had come from Houdini, that made sense.

"It's possible once you learn how to control your own power, you won't feel like it controls you," Houdini's father said. "But either way, you both are coming with us."

"Excellent," Benvolio said, slapping his hands and then rubbing them together vigorously.

His enthusiasm and my mother's fear both felt so misplaced to me, though. Whatever Houdini's parents had in mind, it wasn't what either of them thought.

And I didn't even know what I thought it would be.

The Wizard seemed to share my concern, though. He cleared his throat to catch the attention of the two dragons who had already started fussing over my parents.

"Pardon," the Wizard said. "It's just, I gather time moves differently there than it does here."

"Correct," Houdini put in.

"Yes, so my question is rather... if you take the two of them away, when should we expect their return?" the Wizard asked.

"Well, I would imagine it would be like the return of this dog fellow here," my father said. Then swallowed hard, as he immediately recognized being dismissive of their son was not the best way to get in the two dragons' good graces. "I believe here he is called Houdini?"

"That is my name," Houdini said in a low growl.

"Yes, time flows the way we wish it to," Houdini's mother said. But hastily, even as she herded my mother through the stone archway with a flick of her tail.

There was no visible portal there now, not even the sort we mortals had constructed to connect all of our magical neighborhoods. But my mother vanished midway through her step through the arch all the same.

And I felt a strange stab of emotion. I hadn't gotten a chance to stay goodbye.

Although I had no idea what goodbye there could've been between us.

"We can return to the moment we left, right?" my father asked.

"Quite right," Houdini's father said, then picked up my father in one clawed foot and tossed him unceremoniously through the archway.

My father's shriek of alarm abruptly cut off mid shrill.

"Can," the Wizard said dryly. "Not will."

"But they will be back," Mercutio said. Although whether he was seeking confirmation out of hope or fear, I couldn't tell.

"If they return, they will be so changed you will scarcely recognize them," Houdini's mother said.

"They are being re-educated," Houdini's father said. "They will not be returned until they understand their magic, know how to use it, and have the wisdom to do so for the good of all."

"They're not coming back," Mercutio said, but so low I was sure only I heard him.

"We will get a forewarning?" the Wizard asked mildly.

"I shall be here to keep you up to date," Houdini said.

"You will?" I burst out.

"Of course I will, Tabitha," he said. "I'm your companion. I would never leave you."

"But your parents," I said. "Aren't they closing this rift forever?"

"Indeed, we are," Houdini's mother said. "But only because this is an unnatural rift. It was never meant to be here."

"Curse our curiosity," his father grumbled.

"But there are other ways from our plane to yours?" I asked.

"And I know them all," Houdini assured me. "I can return to my parents whenever I wish to see them, and stay as long as I like. And never be away from your side for longer than I choose."

"Houdini," I said, holding out my arms. He complied, racing across the grass to leap up and lick at my face. "That's the best news I've ever heard."

"I said I would never leave you," he reminded me.

And I believed him. I was so happy, I could lick him back. But I settled for just nuzzling his fur.

Being careful of his ears, of course. They were so sensitive, those ears.

TWENTY-ONE

Houdini said goodbye to his parents. Or, at least, that's what I think was going on. I didn't perceive words or even sounds, really. I kind of felt a breeze, or maybe just smelled it.

The aroma of a high alpine meadow with the wildflowers in fullest bloom. The invigorating coolness of the air blowing through my mind and soul.

That last breath Houdini had showed me back in the Wizard's library inside the Tower what felt like a lifetime ago? That had been his true dragon breath.

It was unspeakably lovely.

Before I had quite noticed it, though, the two older dragons were gone. Houdini stood alone in the center of the clearing, looking up at the broken top of the stone arch.

"It still functions as your usual portal," he said offhandedly as he trotted back to my side. "It just doesn't connect to my parents' home plane. The one beyond order and chaos."

"I have so many questions," I said.

"Don't we all?" Mercutio said. "But maybe we need to start with these two here."

He pointed with his chin towards Cleopatra, still bound up in magic despite my father being in a different dimension now, and then towards Octavio with his hands cuffed by his own manacles. She had a loop of magic binding over her mouth keeping her silent, but Octavio only regarding us all with sullen stares was his own choice.

I had a feeling that would change. Sooner than I'd like.

"They have to tell us about Wendell Gorman," Liam said. "I know it seems like nothing after everything that just happened here, but I want to know."

"It's not nothing. It was murder," I said. "I want an explanation as well."

"We should call the authorities first," Mercutio said. "Whether we can prove anything magical happened to Wendell Gorman or not, we have them dead to rights for violating the terms of Cleopatra Manx's parole."

"Frank and I will do it. We'll go out and find out how the others are doing. Outside this maze," Carlo said. I turned to see the two of them had found the remains of the doorway out of the clearing. A prosaic maze might be easier to navigate after it had mostly burned to the ground, but I had a hunch this magic one would be a different story. They were still going to have to get through it the long way.

"Tell them the danger has passed," Steph said from where he was helping the Wizard settle down on one of the stone benches that flanked the central clearing. "Whatever state the Square is in now, it won't get any worse from now on."

Carlo nodded, and he and Frank started the long trudge through the maze, holding each other tight as they stumbled along.

"You don't know how bad it is?" I asked. "I thought you always sensed everything."

"I think we know for sure now that was never true," the Wizard said with a harsh laugh.

"Bonds have been broken," was all Steph would say. "We'll both need rest before we can start repairing anything."

I didn't like the sound of that.

"It's not getting any worse," Mercutio said. "We can let it stand at that for now."

"Why are you talking like you're in charge?" I asked.

I wasn't being sarcastic or mean. It was a genuine question.

But it seemed to take him by surprise. "Am I?" he asked.

"A little bit," Liam said.

"This one doesn't look like he wants to be helpful at all," I noted, and traded glares with the sullen Octavio before turning to Cleopatra. "Mercutio, can you do what you did to our mother's bindings before? Or does it not work if it was our father's spell?"

"It'll work," he said, then spoke those horribly mangled Latin words a second time.

The loop fell away from Cleopatra's mouth and she bent over and heaved, as if the taste of it had been torture.

But when she was done, she just straightened again, tossing that long blonde hair out of her face, and giving us her most supercilious look.

"The authorities are on their way here, you know," I told her.

She wrinkled her nose in disdain in that way she had, just enough to suggest the emotion, but not so much she would risk wrinkles forming long term.

"I guess it's back to house arrest for me," she said with a dramatic sigh.

"And a matching house arrest for your brother," I said.

I had meant those words a little ironically. House arrest in the Manx family clearly meant no punishment at all. They'd still be moving around the world as much as they liked, doing what they liked. If it meant a little bit more discretion, relying a little bit more on proxies for the really bad stuff, what difference did it make in the end?

I wished Houdini's parents had taken these two with them as well.

I wished the faeries would decide they needed revenge for some transgression or other.

I wished anything but for them to face the justice of my own community. Because that justice wasn't much like justice at all.

And yet, to my surprise, Octavio started ranting.

"House arrest? Everything I did at your bidding, and you're just going to let them put me under house arrest?" he bellowed, stumbling as he charged over to his sister with his hands still bound behind his back.

"Let them?" Cleopatra repeated. "The powers you think I have, little brother. Grow up."

"No, all I did was what you told me to—" he started to say.

"Oh, really?" she barked out a condescending laugh. "Every time you insisted that someone just had to die, that was you doing my bidding? Really?"

"You've gone too soft!" he snarled at her. "This place—"

"I never spent a single night here—"

"—has *destroyed* you—"

"—and what I built here is more than you've *ever*—"

"—too soft to even perceive your plans could not be executed without an actual—oh, I don't know—*execution*—"

"Your blood lust is a weakness, dear brother. A blindness, in fact."

"I'll show you—"

This probably could've gone on for quite a bit longer, the two of them literally in each other's faces. Real dogs gearing up for a fight showed more dignity and less snarling bravado.

But my brother cut them both off. With a single snap of Latin, the gag was back up over Cleopatra's mouth, and her brother had one to match.

"Shall we try this one at a time, maybe?" Mercutio asked me.

"I guess we can start with Cleopatra," I sighed.

He released her gag, and she made another big show of purging herself of the lingering taste on her tongue.

"Your brother killed Wendell Gorman, I gather," I said as she pretended to dry heave. "He wanted to kill Cressida, but you offered him Wendell instead."

"Oh, Wendell offered himself," Cleopatra said. Then she straightened, sweeping her hair back from her face before giving me her most brilliant smile. "It was outside the salon, on the prosaic street. My brother and I were arguing as he was passing by, and he caught her name. There was no getting rid of him after that."

"He heard you plotting murder?" I asked.

Cleopatra laughed. "He heard us plotting a *conversation*," she said. "But her name was like a trigger. He wanted to tell us all about her, how wonderful she was, were we friends of hers?"

"But I don't understand," I said. "Wasn't he looking for *you* the entire time?"

"He was looking for a name he'd seen on paperwork," Cleopatra said. "He was never looking for *me*."

But there was something in the annoyance on her face that was bugging me.

"You sent him looking for you to break down the magic tied up in the prosaic bureaucracy," I said slowly. "But he never met you."

"No," she agreed.

"He didn't know what you looked like."

She tossed a wave of hair back over her shapely shoulder, then said, "No."

"But after he met you—" I started to say.

But Cleopatra was quick to interrupt, as if arguing with her brother had primed her for it. "He still didn't know who I was. I never introduced myself. He was never supposed to *find* me. He was just supposed to be very, very driven about *searching* for me."

"Still, how annoying for you," I said. "He met you—I mean, come on, *you*—and still he was all about Cressida?"

I gestured at the entire form of her with my best version of show model hands. She just scowled at me.

But I knew I was right. She had been annoyed at first. But when Wendell persisted with only being interested in Cressida, that annoyance had edged over into anger.

"I'm not sure your brother acted so much without your consent as you'd have us believe," I said.

Octavio made no sound, because he couldn't, but his eyebrows were making a certain triumphant remark all on their own.

"You killed Wendell Gorman because he annoyed you?" Liam asked with a frown.

"No, I'm guessing Cleopatra already knew what you later found out," I said. "The protections over prosaic bureaucracy had broken down. She didn't need Wendell Gorman asking questions anymore. But you didn't kill him right then and there either, did you? No, he had another use for you. As long as he was there, making himself so handily available and all."

"So you sent him to our father," Mercutio said, stepping forward to stand shoulder to shoulder with me.

It felt kind of... right. Working together like that.

But I put that thought aside, focusing on Cleopatra's face. She was making a show of being impassive, but she was listening.

"You had been plotting with my father for quite some time," Mercutio mused. "The two of you were going to take control of the Square together, weren't you? That was the original plan."

Her face twisted in anger, but only for an instant. Then the impassive mask slipped back into place.

"You were supposed to be the name on the prosaic paperwork, the anchoring name to activate the magic on the deed," Mercutio said. "Your name was on the apartment. But that didn't matter much. That's only in the magical world. It doesn't anchor anything with the prosaic world. But your name was supposed to be on the shop. And that was going to matter. Only you messed up. You got yourself put under house arrest. And my name got put on the lease instead."

Cleopatra said nothing. But a little muscle popped in her jaw. Like she was grinding her teeth, if only ever so slightly.

"Did he speak to you about that decision?" Mercutio asked, clearly rhetorically. "I don't think he did. No, I don't think he spoke to you again after you messed up. Years of planning, down the drain, because you screwed up the assignment of killing a pet."

"It wasn't a cat, it was a matagot," Cleopatra spat out. "Trickier to kill, certainly. But it had to go before the shop could open. It could sense things that would be inconvenient when Benvolio arrived. And it had access to secret libraries, the kind nonhuman creatures maintain. The kind we can't even imagine, let alone get access to."

"I knew it!" Houdini suddenly burst out. He immediately adopted a chagrined look, his ears drooping low. "Sorry. I didn't mean to interrupt. I just... I knew it."

"Miss Snooty Cat knew what you were," I agreed. "Perhaps she even knew who your parents were. But she chose not to tell you."

"I'll never know why, I suppose," he sighed. "But it's still good to know I was right."

"Also, there are libraries maybe you can get to that I can't?" I said with the smallest of grins.

"Wendell Gorman," Liam said, bringing us back on topic.

"Right, you sent him in to... what? Test the protections?" I asked.

"No," my brother said. "She already knew everything she needed to about that."

"Then, why?" I asked.

Cleopatra said nothing.

"To draw out our mother, perhaps?" Mercutio guessed. "You needed her here, didn't you? There was never any opening of that portal without her. But she's tough to find."

"I've always known exactly where she was," Cleopatra said coolly. "I just couldn't get to her. Not on my own. She was always so very paranoid. Ever since she was a little girl. I've seen kittens who were less skittish."

"So—" I started to say, glancing at Liam as I prepared to bring the conversation back around to Wendell Gorman one more time.

But Cleopatra didn't let me finish. Her eyes were locked on my brother's as she said, "No, I couldn't get her on my own. But that's where *you* came in, isn't it?"

And the smile on her face was pure gloating triumph.

She had just lobbed another emotional grenade at me. All she had to do was wait for it to explode.

TWENTY-TWO

I watched all the color drain out of my brother's face. Which, given he had the same moon-pale skin as our mother, was really saying something.

"I never... She doesn't... I *never*... Tabitha?" he stammered helplessly. Cleopatra was still all catty anticipation.

But her grenade had been a dud. As suspicious as I'd ever been of my brother—and for good reason—I wasn't suspicious now.

"Relax," I said, putting a hand on his arm. "She manipulated you. Without your knowledge. By her own design. There's no way she ever trusted you enough to use you as a willing accomplice."

"Thanks?" he said uncertainly.

"So astute, Tabitha Greene," Cleopatra sneered.

"So, wait," Mercutio said, still catching up. "You always knew where she was. So when I was looking for her, the lead that just sort of fell into my lap—"

"Came from me, yes," Cleopatra said. Then added, "Indirectly, of course."

"You knew I was looking for her?" Mercutio pressed.

"My good boy, did you think you were being *discreet*?" she asked with a laugh. "You, the notorious recluse, were suddenly hitting all the right parties. And by 'right' parties, I, of course, mean the sorts of parties the rank and file call the 'wrong' parties."

"Huh?" Liam said.

"Parties the bored rich progeny of the old magical families throw," Mercutio stage-whispered to him. "Because they're bored and rich. And have access to old, dark magic no one should have casual access to."

"Do I even want to know what happens at these parties?" Liam asked.

"No, not really," Mercutio said grimly.

But I wasn't looking at either of them. I was looking at Steph and the Wizard. They were sitting slumped together on the stone bench. Steph, being a little more mobile, was trying to get the Wizard to sip something from a flask, but not having much luck. Still, as always, he felt my eyes on him and looked up at me.

"My brother?" I said to him. It came out way louder and more accusing than I intended.

"What?" Mercutio said, suddenly confused.

"My brother was your spy?" I demanded. Still too loud.

"He was *a* spy," the Wizard said dryly. "He wasn't *my* spy."

"I volunteered," Mercutio said. "I didn't know you guys even knew. I was going to tell you, Tabitha. I mean, I really thought it was going to come up when we talked to our mother. I had a whole speech prepared about the proper way to handle getting mixed up in the old families. Not the way she did it, where you just try to appease them and look out for your own. I wanted to take them down. And not just the Wards. I wanted to take them *all* down."

"Your mother did her best," the Wizard said. But the words seemed to take everything he had left right out of him. He allowed Steph to dose him a little from the flask, then slumped back into weary silence.

"I did warn you," Steph said to my brother. "It was very unlikely they wouldn't suspect what you were up to. And it sounds like they did. Cleopatra made you into her double-agent without you even being aware."

Mercutio had some choice words after hearing that, but he mostly mumbled them to himself under his breath.

"Wendell Gorman," Liam said, with the dogged patience of a man who was willing to keep saying those two words for the rest of his life.

"You didn't need to kill him," Steph said when Cleopatra persisted in saying nothing. "You weren't testing the spells because you already knew how to get prosaics inside. You use the loopholes all the time just to run your shop."

"Or you did, when it was your shop," I put in. Just because I felt like being a little catty myself for a change.

"And you didn't need to send him in to draw Serena out," Steph went on. "Mercutio is wrong about that."

"Would you believe I sent him inside in the sincere hope that doing so would get him away from my bloodthirsty brother?" she asked.

"No," Liam and I said, at once and together.

"Not really," Mercutio said.

Cleopatra blinked, like our words had truly caught her by surprise.

"Well, I did," she said. "And yes, I knew how to get him inside, but I didn't use my salon. I guess I could feel the place was already turning on me. There was no way that man should be quite so taken with Cressida Cade."

"She's a lovely person," I said, almost defensively.

Cleopatra rolled her eyes.

"Where did he get in from?" Liam asked, still laser-focused on the actual mission.

"The coffeeshop," Cleopatra said. "Titus barely maintains the spells there. His wife did most of that work when she was around, and now that she isn't? Elephants could charge into the Square through his coffeeshop."

I looked over at Steph to see what he thought of this, but he was just slumped with his face in his hands. Although it was possible he had already been in that position before she mentioned anything about the coffeeshop. I had never seen him so dead-on-his-feet tired.

I mean, he was too exhausted to take the Wizard home. That told me a lot.

But I didn't need Liam's prompting this time to turn my attention back to the interrogation in progress.

"So Gorman went in through the coffeeshop, then up to my father's apartment. Looking for you. But my father sent him off on his own back through the Square," I said. "Back to the coffeeshop?"

"No, he got lost," Cleopatra said with a sigh. "He was just sort of bumping around at the base of the Tower. But no one came out to see what he was up to. I watched him like that for the better part of an hour."

"So you went inside," I guessed.

"I wanted to send just my brother, but I knew that would be a mistake," she said. "So we both went and got him. But he was deeply freaked out by then. There was no way I could just take him outside the Square and let him go. I mean, I was taking down the protections of this place, but in a surgical manner. Layer by layer. Not all at once with one loony running around screaming 'look at that totally anachronistic tower over there!' and having everyone just see it."

"What did you do?" Mercutio asked.

"We brought him to the portal," Cleopatra said.

"But he wasn't killed there," I said.

"No, not where we left him," Cleopatra agreed. "We brought him through the portal to... Well, it doesn't matter. That was my brother's call. He had friends with a portal of their own—"

"Rich, steeped in old, dark magic friends," Mercutio guessed.

But she ignored him. "—friends who not only had ways of dispatching prosaics quickly and without a trace, but had... shall we say, a penchant for it?"

"Please don't," Mercutio groaned.

Liam just dead-eye stared at Cleopatra. As if he had no fear of her at all. Which, even bound up as she was, was a little irrational for a prosaic.

But also, kind of admirable.

"You let your brother and his friends kill Wendell Gorman, because his use to you as a tool had come to an end. Had, in fact, driven him irredeemably insane. And then you just chucked him out onto the grass and went home?"

"I *was* under house arrest," Cleopatra said with a creepy sort of smile. "I have to check in periodically. My time was up."

"Speaking of time being up," Mercutio said, then spoke the words that replaced the gag over her mouth.

I'd really have to talk to him later about his Latin. It was making me cringe, every single time.

Mercutio walked over to the darkly scowling form of Octavio Manx. He removed the gag, and we all subjected ourselves to a full minute of expletive-laden threats interlaced with bouts of inarticulate but clearly rage-filled screaming.

Then my brother spoke his spell again, and we were once more in the blissful silence of a cold October night.

"That's what I thought he'd say," my brother said at last.

None of us laughed.

"Is she right?" Liam asked. "Is it just house arrest for both of them again?"

I was about to express my own frustration but also inevitable acceptance of that fact when my brother said, "No."

Steph perked up at that. Or, at least, as much as he was able to. "What do you mean?" he asked.

"I mean no," he said again. "Not if I have anything to say about it, anyway."

"Your work as a spy gives you leverage with the courts?" I asked. Deeply skeptically.

But Mercutio just blushed. "No. I mean, maybe? But no. I'm talking about me. I guess we haven't had it confirmed yet, but it seems pretty likely that our grandfather and great-grandfather are both dead. Murdered, by the Unveiled Guild. And our father, even if he hadn't been removed from the family line, is definitely not available at the moment."

"But the Ward family is huge," I said. "We must have tons of cousins."

"Not really," Mercutio said. "I mean, not close ones. That's why they insisted I have the Ward name. I'm next in line. I guess, as of a few hours ago, I'm the patriarch."

Liam gave his former roommate a look like he didn't know quite what to say.

Weirdly, that look spoke for all of us.

"I know this is going to be a headache, all the legal and financial wizards I'm going to have to consult before I even know what's going on, let alone what my actual powers are," Mercutio said. But then his voice grew hard and brittle as he looked from Octavio to Cleopatra and then back again. "But this I swear. With every bit of power that does come with the Ward name, I will do everything I can to make sure the two of you never see sunlight or moonlight again. Drink it up now, Manxs. This harvest moon is the last one you'll ever see."

Octavio turned his back on that moon at once, preferring to scowl at the outline of the bookshop beyond.

But Cleopatra looked up into the sky with something like real regret. She, anyway, seemed to think my brother could do everything he swore to do.

Which made one of us. But it was nice that Mercutio wanted to try.

"I'm sorry, Tabitha," he said. "For one fleeting moment, I thought there was a way to get our father to see me, to really see me. But all he ever saw was a connection to his own father and grandfather, a connection he resented I guess more than I knew."

"I'm sorry. I can only imagine how that felt," I said. Which was true. I had never longed for a relationship with our father.

But I knew he had.

"I thought doing what he asked was a path to him accepting me, but that was stupid. *I* was stupid," he said with sincere emphasis. "And I hurt you, the only person who ever *did* really see me. Like I said, I was stupid."

"Well," I said, and tried to summon up a smile. "I mean, I already knew that."

"I know everything I've done since doesn't make up for how I betrayed you," he said. When I started to sputter a response, he waved his hands to make me stop. "No, seriously. I *know* that. Because they were never intended to. Spying on the dark families, helping the authorities build cases against five of them, including the Wards. All of that was about me. I needed to change how I saw myself first."

"Finding our mother was a little bit about me, though, right?" I asked.

"Sure, bring that up," he grumbled. "My latest spectacular failure. So I'm still at square one in rebuilding our relationship. But it's not zero, right?"

"Right," I gave in with a sigh. "And if you can truly see these two brought to real justice, I'm prepared to call that square... I don't know. A thousand?"

"How many squares are there?" Liam asked with the first flash of something almost like his usual humor back in his eyes.

"Infinite," Mercutio said, throwing an arm around his old roommate's shoulders. "But it's the journey, not the destination, right?"

And, well. I had to agree. Everything in life was a journey.

Which was why it was so important to pick the right companions. They made the infinite journey so much better.

They made it worth the effort to just keep going.

TWENTY-THREE

Sadly, I hadn't been wrong before about why Steph and the Wizard were still sitting on that stone bench. They, physically, couldn't do more than that.

But after the Wizard had taken another few sips from Steph's flask, Liam and I each took one of the Wizard's frail arms and gently helped him to his feet. Mercutio, after a momentary awkwardness, reached out a hand to Steph. And after another, even longer awkward moment, Steph took it and let my brother pull him to his feet.

Then the five of us, with Houdini trotting beside me, made our way back out of the smoking remains of the hedge.

"It will be all right, Tabitha," the Wizard said, as if he could sense my sorrow coming off of me in waves. "The damage was extensive, and it will take time to recover. But the roots are strong. The hedge will return."

I hoped he was right.

When we finally emerged from the smoldering remains of the southern-most entrance into the hedge maze, I saw what had to be every single resident of the Square gathered around the yard in front of the bookshop, waiting for us.

Liam made sure I had the Wizard on my own before running to catch Audrey up in a tight, spinning hug. The momentary look of alarm on her face when she saw just how soot-covered he was faded when she realized that underneath all of that black dust, he was perfectly fine.

The Wizard signaled to me that he needed to rest for a minute, but now that we were well clear of the hedge, the others started to draw closer. I saw my uncles in a throng of people discussing something intently. Barnardo was close by, with Sia in his arms. He had thrown a very old beige robe over sweats and a T-shirt, and was standing on the frost-covered grass in his socks.

Everyone had gotten out of bed to join the cause, apparently.

But they must have succeeded. Even as I looked around, I saw no apparent damage to any structure of the Square around us. Just the hedge maze was burned. The fire had gone no farther.

Then I saw two of the crowd approaching us: Titus Bloom and Violenta Court. Violenta Court was always hard to miss, being six feet tall and nearly as wide but usually decked out in the most feminine of gauzy, flowing layers with lots of tinkling jewelry.

Of course, having rushed out of bed to join the fight, she wasn't wearing any of the jewelry at the moment. But her nightgown and matching robe were pink satin with white and rose embroidered details. And her cotton candy pink hair with its rose tips was in the same Marie Antoinette updo she always wore, if currently covered by some sort of silk sleeping cap.

Or, more like a sack. It was a lot of hair. I confess, I had always assumed it was a wig.

"The authorities told us all to wait out here," Titus said as he approached us. He was wearing his pajamas, the same as all the others. But, I realized, with a start, they were the exact same pajamas he had been wearing the night Agatha Mirken had died. It wasn't the day we'd met, but it had still been a rather significant day in both our lives.

And here was another one we'd never forget.

"As well they should," the Wizard said. "The damage was extensive, and the hedge is not yet recovered enough not to be dangerous. Particularly for younger, less experienced magical users. They may get lost and never find their way back out again."

"Ever?" Violenta Court asked.

"I wouldn't want to venture a guess," the Wizard said. "But it's only for a few days. Let the hedge recover a bit, and it will serve us as merrily as it ever has. But the portal will, sadly, be completely inaccessible until then."

"No more questions just now, though," I interrupted something Titus had been about to say. "The Wizard needs to rest. Seriously."

"I can well imagine," Titus said grimly. "I'm dead on my feet myself. But at least I had my new troll companion at my side the entire time. Never would've made it through without him."

I frowned my puzzlement at him, but before he could explain, Violenta said, "Oh, yes. I adore my cloud of pixies. They are simply charming."

"Are we talking about—?" I started to ask.

"The shop spirits," Audrey finished for me as she and Liam joined our little group. I smiled at the sight; they were both pretty much equally covered in soot now.

"They're all around us," Liam said. "Didn't you notice?"

I looked around, and flushed in embarrassment. There really were spirits all throughout the crowd, now that I was looking properly. I saw Inanna, towering over Cressida and Phoebe. And there was, indeed, a little ugly-cute troll thing standing mostly behind Titus, holding on to the leg of his pajamas like a shy toddler meeting a stranger.

And when Violenta gave her head a shake, a cloud of little winged pixies flew out of her hair cap to float all around her in zipping, laughing loop-de-loops.

"How did you get them to last so long?" I asked.

Although my grasp of the passing of time was, admittedly, strained. It felt like five minutes had gone by inside that maze. But it also felt like a million years. Surely the actual amount of time past was longer than the lifetime of a tea light, though.

But Audrey was smiling at me again in that way that said she had something to show me. Then she held out her hand.

Sitting on her palm was a little tea light candle.

"Okay," I said slowly, not sure what I was missing.

"It's battery-operated," she told me, and turned it over to flip it on. Now it glowed on the palm of her hand with a very convincing flame-like light. "Liam gave me the idea."

"Of course he did," I said, and Liam flushed.

"The spirits last longer now, although not forever," Audrey said as she tucked the light back in her pocket. "But everyone knows the spell now. A few had trouble with it, but I think in a few days everyone will be able to pull it off without too much of my help."

"Wait, so everyone wants permanent shop spirits?" I asked.

"Everyone," Titus said before Audrey could even open her mouth. "These things saved us. They literally saved us."

"And the Square," Violenta said. "Things were breaking apart. We had some scary moments. Particularly after that fire started. I truly thought that was going to be the end. And there was my emergency exit, just where I had found it last week. A new alley between my shop and the Abergavennies's corner store. Like it was calling to me."

"You were never seriously going to run away," Titus said, as if the very idea it might be true not only was unthinkable, but was downright offensive.

"I had already been to the salon and the coffeeshop as well as the bakery and corner store," Audrey said. "I helped Violenta manifest her cloud of pixies, and they were helping to hold things together even before we knew for sure the hedge was on fire."

"You went to every shop?" I asked.

"Even your father's," she said. Then she shuddered, as if the memory disturbed her. "He wasn't in, obviously. And it took a bit of convincing to get the old sea captain thing that lurks there to manifest for me. And then he insisted he would only protect his bit of the Square. He wouldn't come out to join forces with the others."

"We didn't need him," Violenta said as she lifted the edge of her cap to let her suddenly sleepy pixies back inside.

"And the teashop?" I asked.

"She wants us to call her Miss Meow, and I think Barnardo is half in love with her," Audrey said. "She was here for the fight, but she's gone back inside the shop now. I think she's making tea."

"Of course she is," I said. "Let's bring the Wizard there. Whatever is in Steph's flask, I'm sure it's something of your creation, or Agatha's."

"Yes," the Wizard said, stirring out of his torpor if just for a moment. "Agatha's tea. Just the thing."

We started towards the teashop when I realized I had lost track of Mercutio and Steph. They had been with us when we emerged from the hedge maze, but they had kept moving when the Wizard and I had stopped.

Then I saw them both, standing with my uncles.

And what appeared to be a third uncle. My uncles had one of those sorts of marriages where they just resemble each other more and more every year. Same portly stature, same thinning gray hair. Same taste in elbow-patched cardigans.

Then I realized I hadn't gained a third uncle. Because that extra form had a shimmer to it.

It was the spirit of the bookshop.

I longed to run over to it, to throw my arms around it in the biggest of bear hugs. I longed to thank it effusively for everything it had ever done for me. Every book it had left in my path just when I needed to find it. Every glass of cold lemonade or cup of hot tea that appeared just when I was getting parched in the deep throes of research.

But the Wizard was still leaning heavily on me as we walked, and I didn't want to leave his side.

But that was okay. There'd be time enough later.

There'd be all the time in the world.

"What happens now?" Liam asked the Wizard.

It was odd how free Liam was in his manner with the Wizard. This was the first time they'd ever met, after all. And the Wizard tended to be intimidating, even to other wizards.

But of course Liam, as a prosaic, didn't know any of that. Liam was just interacting with what he saw: an old man who was in need of aid, but also the old man who was still the one in charge.

"Now?" the Wizard said, looking around as if seeing the Square for the first time.

"Yes. You said the hedge would grow back, but what about the rest of it?" Liam asked.

"Oh, things have very much changed, haven't they?" the Wizard said musingly.

I looked around again too, but whatever the Wizard had just seen remained invisible to my eyes.

"He means the spells," Steph said, suddenly at my side. "Everything we've done... well, everything the Wizard has done to maintain this place, that's all changed now. With the shop spirits being conjured by the shop owners, it takes almost all the load off of the two of us."

"Really?" I said.

"They have to work together, and we'll still be needed for the parts of the structure that connect *everything*, but mostly it will be a group effort now," Steph said. "More work for everyone else, but less work for the two of us."

"Did you *want* less work?" I asked the Wizard as gingerly as I could.

The Wizard just laughed. "Don't worry, young Tabitha. I have plenty still to fill my time. More than enough to fill ten lifetimes, if truth be told."

"But it will be more research now," Steph said with a fond smile. "More studying and experimenting."

"More being a recluse?" I added.

I was being whimsical, but the Wizard suddenly drew in on himself as if in sadness.

"No. No, I don't think so," he said softly. "No, that does not serve anyone, does it?"

"Well, the point of it is sort of the opposite," I said.

"Hm," he said, which I couldn't parse at all. But then he said, "No, no more hiding away for me. I do believe the time has come to open my Tower up to everyone."

"Everyone?" Liam asked in wide-eyed shock.

"Well, everyone in the Square," the Wizard quickly amended.

"Oh," Liam said. He clearly took that to mean the Wizard would only allow in magical people. Which would make sense. Magical books and magical experiments would seem to require magical users.

But the Wizard reached out a gnarled hand to pat Liam awkwardly on the shoulder. "Everyone in the Square, young man. Don't think I don't know you and young Audrey share that apartment that used to be Agatha's."

Liam blushed furiously but said nothing.

"That makes you one of us," I told him as we pulled open the doors and went inside the teashop.

Where Miss Meow waited with two covered mugs on a tray. The Wizard gave her a nod of thanks, then lifted the lid off of one of the mugs.

I had smelled better aromas wafting off of roadkill.

But the Wizard just shrugged with a grim sort of smile, picked up the cup, and downed the contents as quickly as humanly possible.

"Ooh, the effects are quite rapid," he said, blinking repeatedly as he drunkenly fumbled getting the cup back on the tray.

Miss Meow guided the tray under his tumbling cup just in time to catch it neatly. Then she presented the remaining covered mug to Steph.

"Bottoms up," the Wizard said. "Perhaps Miss Audrey will help me back to the Tower?"

"Are you sure you don't need me to—" Steph started to offer.

But the Wizard waved him away. "Agatha Mirken's grandniece surely has all the power required to get me safely tucked away in bed. Shall we?"

Audrey gave me a single nervous smile. She had never been inside of the Tower before.

But then she looped her arm through the Wizard's, and in the blink of an eye, they were both gone.

"Perhaps I should get closer to a bed before taking this myself," Steph said, sniffing at the contents of his cup.

"A wise idea," Miss Meow said.

And in the next blink of my eye, the entire teashop was gone. There was no sign of Miss Meow and her tea tray, or of soot-covered Liam.

Just me, and Steph, and Houdini, up in my bedroom over the bookshop.

The bedroom where I had spent many long hours of sleep-filled recovery myself. And even as Steph sat down at the edge of my bed, Houdini was already turning around and around, making his dog nest out of the blanket at the foot of the bed.

"I might sleep for a bit here," Steph warned me as he raised the cup to his lips.

"Go ahead," I told him. "I'll be here when you wake up. Just like you always are for me."

He just smiled at me, and drank down the foul-smelling tea.

And I settled into the chair that was usually his sentry station, the one between the bed and the window.

The French window which now stood completely intact in that space.

Actually, no. It wasn't the same as before. It was larger. I wouldn't have to stoop down to step through it. It opened in two side-by-side doors. And the balcony beyond had grown larger too. Large enough for a table and four chairs.

There was even a dog bed in the corner, just perfect for Houdini.

I mean, I already knew the bookshop loved me.

But now I really, *really* knew.

TWENTY-FOUR

Snow came early that year. Very early. Like, the day after Halloween early.

Which, as the other residents in the Square kept telling me, was nothing like the blizzard that had struck on Halloween in 1991. This was just a dusting of flakes, barely enough to cover the leaves on the ground. That had been epic.

Trust me. They brought it up a lot.

It might not have seemed like a lot of snow to them, who'd apparently been through worse. But it was a lot to Houdini and me.

Or, I guess, to Houdini.

I had once attended a magical academy hidden on the continent of Antarctica, after all.

But this was his first winter. And, as it turned out, he was only kind of, partly, a white dragon. Sure, he could emit a breath of frost if he wanted to.

But he wasn't as immune to cold as he thought.

"Agatha got these booties for you just for this reason," I said as I tried for the fourth time to get one of said booties on Houdini's front paw.

"I don't need them!" Houdini insisted with all the stubborn surety of a toddler.

"Fine," I said. "Go outside barefoot. See how it feels."

"I will," he said, and trotted down the stairs from my bedroom with his corkscrew of a tail held high above him.

"You'll be back," I said, but only to myself. I gathered the four boots—together with a cute dog sweater than was made to look like a cable-knit sweater over a flannel shirt which I hadn't even started trying to talk Houdini into wearing even though it was so very cute —and shoved it all into the cargo pocket of my pants.

Then I pulled on my own shoes—my usual Converse sneakers rather than the clunky winter boots I had dug out of the very depths of my suitcase—and admitted that it wasn't like I couldn't see Houdini's point. I would wear sneakers through wet snow until it became physically unbearable to continue doing so. And I wouldn't switch to boots until the minute I absolutely had to.

After tying my shoes, I checked my hair briefly in the mirror by my door. As always, this was less about my appearance in a cosmetic sense and more a check for any sign of my power returning.

But my curls were soft and manageable. And I tried not to be disappointed that I had rolled out of bed looking good.

My life had enough sources of irony in it.

I said a brief hello to both of my uncles sharing coffee and a crossword in their galley kitchen, but only took a heel of yesterday's bread for myself before running down to my nook in the heart of the bookshop.

I felt his presence beside me on the stairs, the ghostly form of my third uncle. He preferred if I didn't acknowledge him too much. It made him feel too self-conscious. But I could tell by the way he was following me that he was letting me know someone was waiting for me inside my nook.

He might not like to speak, but he would never again let me be blindsided by anyone in the safety of his space.

"Thank you, Uncle Weal & Woe," I whispered. I felt him fade away then, but I knew he wasn't going far.

He would be back in a flash if I should need him.

I strolled into my nook to find my brother there with his back to me, waiting at the window that looked out over Minneapolis, with his feet planted wide and his hands folded behind his back. Half military officer at parade rest, half making sure to communicate to whomever would want to know that he wasn't going to touch anything without getting permission first.

The bookshop had been less eager to forgive him than I had. I gather there had been a few shocks of static electricity when Mercutio brushed up against the wrong things.

Or, really, anything at all.

"How goes the life of the scion?" I asked him.

He turned around and gave me a sour face. "Don't ask."

"Okay," I said, and skipped over to my table to dig through the stacks of books waiting for me there. "I found a couple of things that might come in handy for you and your financial wizards," I said. I picked up a book I thought was what I was looking for, but the spine declared it to be a text about magical calculus, and I set it aside.

Although that was a project I definitely wanted to get back to.

"Here it is," I said at last, and handed him a thin, leather-bound chapbook and a heftier tome bound in... well, let's just hope it was also leather.

"And these books are about accounting," Mercutio said, wrinkling his nose in distaste as he took the both of them from me.

"I guess it's not surprising there aren't a lot of books that cover the crossover of dark magic and accounting," I said.

But then I thought about it again and added, "Or maybe it is surprising. Don't they all lie about money?"

"Depends on how you define dark magic," Mercutio said. "These should help tremendously, I'm sure. Thank you."

"And the basic Latin guide I lent you?" I asked.

"You needed it back?" he asked. Too eagerly.

"No, have you been working on it?" I asked him.

"I don't have the ear for vowel sounds that you do," he said almost testily.

"This is Latin," I told him. "Not Danish."

"Danish is—" he started to ask.

But I was already there. I had tapped in a quick internet search on my phone and showed him the screen with all the vowels there. The basics, plus a few extra ones with two letters smashed together, or an 'a' with a circle on top of it.

Only, was that the most extreme case language?

"Doesn't even have umlauts," I said, mostly to myself.

"I get your point," he said before I could start another search. I put my phone away agreeably.

"No excuses, then," I said.

"Only a general lack of time," he said. "The state of affairs in the Ward family has been a mess for generations. It's a lot to clean up, just me on my own."

"You have my sympathy," I said. But with just the hint of an edge. Not anger, just defining a boundary. Just enough to remind him of every other time he'd asked for my help and I had turned him down.

I would never, ever consider myself a Ward.

Not that I wasn't proud of what my brother was doing. If he achieved even half of what he was setting out to do, by the time he was our father's age, the name of Ward would have an entirely different reputation.

Still, that mission was not mine. Admirable though it was.

"Whatever you're up against, I'm sure you can handle it," I said, and relented a little to pull him into a tight hug. "And if you need me to do more research for you, I'm always happy to help out."

"I know," he said as he returned the hug. "And I do appreciate it. I still hope when things calm down a little, we can try working on magic together again. Houdini must have some ideas of how our chaos and order should flow."

"I'm sure he does," I said cheerily. But then I snapped my fingers. I didn't have to explain that gesture. He knew what it meant.

Still no spark. Everything I had pulled from that portal I had blasted straight up into the sky.

Making the prosaic news, actually.

But not a bit of it had remained inside me. I had been thoroughly tapped out all over again. And after nearly a month, I remained an empty well.

And I was perfectly happy with that.

"Do you think they'll ever come back?" my brother asked. He obviously meant our parents.

"I don't know," I admitted.

"Do you want them to?"

I gave that a longer moment's thought. But the answer was the same in the end. "I don't know."

We stood in silence for a moment, but it was a nice kind of silence. Like we were sharing our feelings without having to actually speak them out loud. We understood each other.

But that moment came to an end, as they all do.

"I should get going," Mercutio said.

"Not staying for breakfast?" I asked. "Everyone would love to see you."

"And I would love to see them, but I have back-to-back meetings all day," he said. "Tell Liam and everyone hello from me."

"Even Steph?" I taunted him.

"Even Steph," he said, and almost sounded like he meant it. "I don't hate your boyfriend!" he tossed back over his shoulder as he walked away from my nook.

And then he was gone.

I dug through the stacks again until I had that calculus volume back in my hands. I found a fresh journal waiting on the far side of the table and put them both together in a stack in front of my customary chair.

I would dig into that after I got back from breakfast.

And I was sure by the time my shift at the bookshop started after lunchtime, I would be *so* ready to take a break. Magical calculus was the marathon running of brain activities. Or maybe more like an iron man competition.

Super strenuous and exhausting.

But when I ran into trouble, as I knew I would, I had a boyfriend who excelled at it. And was very good at explaining things to me. He also just happened to have his evenings free all the time now.

I had created the shop spirit spell for Audrey, but I couldn't deny I was the one who had benefited the most from it. And was still benefiting. Every single day.

Although the Wizard in his Tower was enjoying his freedom quite a bit as well. Or so I heard from Liam, his most constant companion these days.

I went down the stairs to the main level of the bookshop, but rather than take the secret door to the teashop, I went outside into the cold November day.

The snow on the ground really was a piddling amount, but it was honestly quite pretty. It had fallen overnight, and now it was shining like broken crystals from fallen chandeliers in the light of the rising sun.

And off to my left I could see the branches of the hedges literally shaking the snow off of themselves. They were growing so fast it almost felt like you could take a seat on one of the stone benches and just watch it happen. It wasn't actually quite that fast—I knew because I'd tried it—but they had already recovered half of their impressive height.

All that without the warmth of summer and barely a smattering of rain.

As I was looking in that direction, I saw a flash of light. Someone had just hopped into the Square through the portal. Or maybe a few someones. People were coming and going as briskly as ever now. And of course the mail always went through.

"I do not regret this," Houdini said in my mind. I looked down to see him shivering in front of me, one damp paw up in the air as if he wanted to press it to his chest but was afraid that would just make his chest cold.

"Of course you don't," I said and bent to scoop him up. He eagerly let me tuck him inside the front of my hoodie. I pressed the folds of warm cotton over each of his paws in turn until I was sure all the snow had melted away, then zipped up the front so that he was cradled close to my chest.

"Thank you, Tabitha," he said, still trembling. He had more chihuahua in him than he liked to admit.

"You know, you could always turn into your dragon form," I told him. "We had a hairy few weeks there, but it's perfectly safe now."

Which, we all guessed, was probably finally true. Mostly, the outside world was back to ignoring us. The first few days after the hedge burned down had been filled with a lot of crazy stories in the prosaic papers, but most of the locals chalked it all up to the usual late October scary season stuff.

Ghost stories. Witches gathering under the full moon. That kind of thing. And if all the stories kept happening in the same little block of St. Anthony, that was just some journalist's lack of imagination, right?

Not that things were completely back to how they'd been before. We get a lot more prosaics accidentally going through one of the shops and into the Square beyond than we used to. Mostly the kind of people who are more sensitive to magic than others.

It was like our neighborhood had become a sort of beacon, luring them in.

But we knew how to get them out again safely. And without drama. It was a group effort, but the whole neighborhood was on board.

They all got out safely, and everyone inside the Square was safe. Definitely, the lack of murders was my favorite thing about this new version of the Square.

"I'm hungry," Houdini said, poking his nose back out from the front of my hoodie. "Audrey promised a new recipe for dog treats today."

"Did she?" I said as I headed towards the teashop door. "You know, you never told me what you ate when you were with your parents. What *do* dragons eat? Raw meat? Cooked meat?"

"There is a sort of waft of air that is nutritively filling," Houdini said. But I could hear the disdain in his voice.

"You didn't like it?" I guessed.

"It was all right," he said. "It wasn't *food*."

"And here I thought you wanted to stay in this dimension just for me," I said as I planted a kiss between his ears.

"It was *mostly* for you," he said. "But it was also for the food."

"I'm just glad you're here," I told him.

The bell over the door jangled as we pushed our way into the teashop. And there were my friends, all gathered together around a fresh pot of tea still wrapped in its cozy towel. Liam had a plate of savory scones in his hands—something with flecks of herbs and dark orange bits of cheese—and Audrey had another of sweet scones. I smelled cranberry and orange. But perhaps that was coming from the tea?

Whichever. I knew it would be perfection.

"Tabitha!" Barnardo said with his usual heavy dose of enthusiasm. "Have you heard the latest bit of news?"

"Not until you tell me," I said as I unzipped my hoodie and let Houdini out. He immediately trotted over to Sia and touched his nose to hers in hello.

"Apparently it's about Titus and Violenta," Audrey said in a tone that said she was warning me what was to come.

"Kind of the logical conclusion if you saw the two of them together the night of the dragons," Liam added.

"I kind of saw them together?" I allowed as I slid into the chair next to Steph. "But you tell it," I added. Because Barnardo was going to burst if he didn't get to spill all he had seen in every glorious detail.

And I just let his words wash over me as I watched Audrey and Liam whispering together, debating the timing on the tea. Liam nodded his agreement and Audrey started filling all our cups.

Bergamot. Her favorite. Every time I smelled it, I thought of her. My best friend.

And Liam, my oldest friend, always right by her side.

And I could never forget Barnardo, still regaling us all with more details than we wanted about what sounded like, frankly, a rather chaste and adorably awkward first date. And a sweet moment that really should've been theirs alone, but Barnardo never saw it that way.

Then I looked at my boyfriend beside me. Steph, who had never looked better. His skin had a rosy color to it that really brought out the golden highlights in his brown eyes.

I could stare into those eyes forever.

I mean, literally. I could. I had the time.

And, finally, so did he.

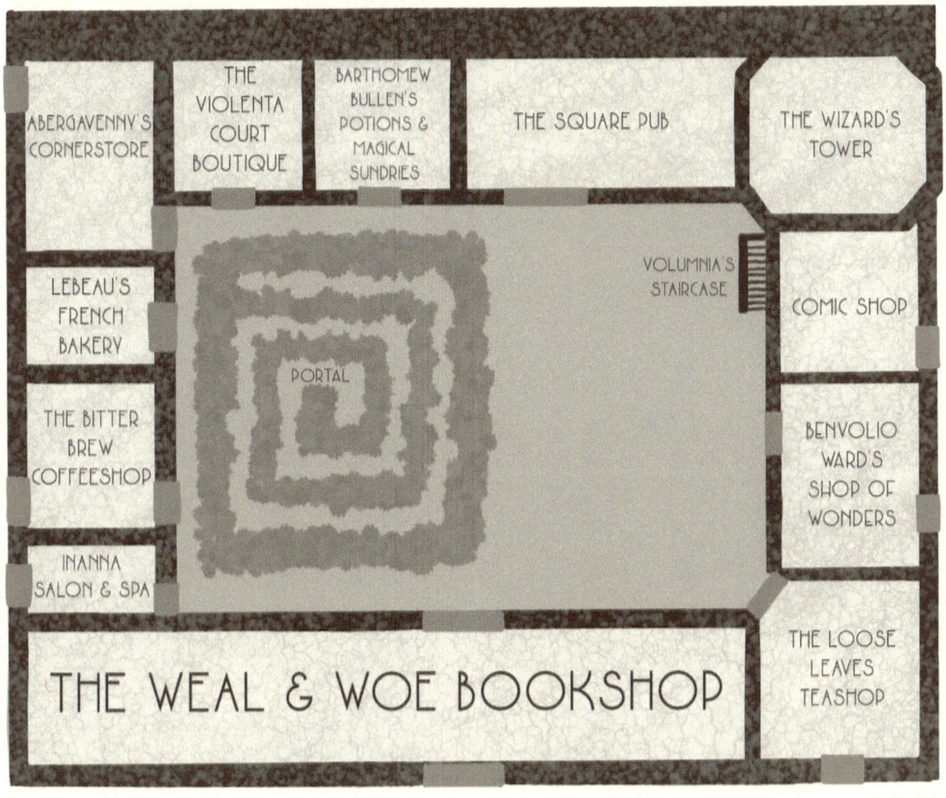

ABERGAVENNY'S CORNERSTORE
THE VIOLENTA COURT BOUTIQUE
BARTHOMEW BULLEN'S POTIONS & MAGICAL SUNDRIES
THE SQUARE PUB
THE WIZARD'S TOWER
LEBEAU'S FRENCH BAKERY
VOLUMNIA'S STAIRCASE
COMIC SHOP
PORTAL
THE BITTER BREW COFFEESHOP
BENVOLIO WARD'S SHOP OF WONDERS
INANNA SALON & SPA
THE WEAL & WOE BOOKSHOP
THE LOOSE LEAVES TEASHOP

THE WITCHES THREE COZY MYSTERIES

In case you missed it, check out Charm School, the first book in the complete Witches Three Cozy Mystery Series!

Amanda Clarke thinks of herself as perfectly ordinary in every way. Just a small-town girl who serves breakfast all day in a little diner nestled next to the highway, nothing but dairy farms for miles around. She fits in there.

But then an old woman she never met dies, and Amanda was named in her will. Now Amanda packs a bag and heads to the big city, to Miss Zenobia Weekes' Charm School for Exceptional Young Ladies. And it's not in just any neighborhood. No, she finds herself on Summit Avenue in St. Paul, a street lined with gorgeous old houses, the former homes of lumber barons, railroad millionaires, even the writer F. Scott Fitzgerald. Why, Amanda can practically hear the jazz music still playing across the decades.

Scratch that. The music really, literally, still plays in the backyard of the charm school. Because the house stretches across time itself. Without a witch to protect this tear in the fabric of the world, anything can spill over. Like music.

Or like murder.

Charm School, the first book in the complete Witches Three Cozy Mystery Series!

THE VIKING WITCH COZY MYSTERIES

In case you missed it, check out Body at the Crossroads, the first book in the Viking Witch Cozy Mystery Series!

When her mother dies after a long illness, Ingrid Torfa must sell the family home to cover the medical bills. Her career as a book illustrator not yet exactly launched, Ingrid faces two options: live in her battered old Volkswagen, or go back to her mother's small town in northern Minnesota.

The small town that still haunts her dreams more than a decade since she last visited it. Or rather, not the town but the grandmother.

All of the drawings she fills notebooks with witches and the trolls that do their bidding? Not as whimsical in her nightmares as she sketches them in the bright light of day.

If not for her beloved cat Mjolner, living in the Volkswagen just might tempt her.

But the cat wants four walls and a door, so north she goes. And finds trouble in the form of a dead body before she even finds her grandmother's little town. How much can a town of stoic fishermen possibly be hiding?

As Ingrid is about to find out, quite a lot.

Body at the Crossroads, the first book in the Viking Witch Cozy Mystery Series!

ALSO FROM RATATOSKR PRESS

The Ritchie and Fitz Sci-Fi Murder Mysteries starts with Murder on the Intergalactic Railway.

For Murdina Ritchie, acceptance at the Oymyakon Foreign Service Academy means one last chance at her dream of becoming a diplomat for the Union of Free Worlds. For Shackleton Fitz IV, it represents his last chance not to fail out of military service entirely.

Strange that fate should throw them together now, among the last group of students admitted after the start of the semester. They had once shared the strongest of friendships. But that all ended a long time ago.

But when an insufferable but politically important woman turns up murdered, the two agree to put their differences aside and work together to solve the case.

Because the murderer might strike again. But more importantly, solving a murder would just have to impress the dour colonel who clearly thinks neither of them belong at his academy.

Murder on the Intergalactic Railway, the first book in the Ritchie and Fitz Sci-Fi Murder Mysteries, available everywhere books are sold.

FREE EBOOK!

Like exclusive, free content?

If you'd like to receive "A Collection of Witchy Prequels", a free collection of short story prequels to the Witches Three Cozy Mystery and Viking Witch Cozy Mystery series, as well as other free stories throughout the year, go to my website CateMartin.com to subscribe to my newsletter! This eBook is exclusively for newsletter subscribers and will never be sold in stores. Check it out!

ABOUT THE AUTHOR

Cate Martin has written stories which have appeared in the **Mystery, Crime and Mayhem** quarterly magazine as well as in the annual **Holiday Spectacular** Advent calendar of holiday stories. She is also the author of three witch mystery series: **The Witches Three Cozy Mysteries**, and **The Viking Witch Cozy Mysteries** and **The Weal & Woe Bookshop Witch Mysteries**. She currently lives in Minneapolis, Minnesota. You can learn more about her work at Cate-Martin.com.

Also by Cate Martin

The Witches Three Cozy Mystery Series

Charm School

Work Like a Charm

Third Time is a Charm

Old World Charm

Charm his Pants Off

Charm Offensive

The Witches Three Cozy Mysteries Books 1-3

The Witches Three Cozy Mysteries Books 4-6

The Viking Witch Cozy Mystery Series

Body at the Crossroads

Death Under the Bridge

Murder on the Lake

Killing in the Village Commons

Bloodshed in the Forest

Corpse in the Mead Hall

Slaying on the Lake Shore

Bones by the Forest Road

Sacrifice Behind the Falls

Body Under the Café

Assassination in the Glade

Bewitchment After the Storm

Predator in the Lanes (available January 14, 2025 direct from me or February 11, 2025 in stores everywhere)

The Viking Witch Cozy Mysteries Books 1-3

The Viking Witch Cozy Mysteries Books 4-6

The Weal & Woe Bookshop Witch Mystery Series

The Teashop Terror

The Salon & Spa Scandal

The Bookseller Blunder

The Entrepreneur Enigma

The Novelty Shop Nightmare

The Courtyard Conundrum

www.ingramcontent.com/pod-product-compliance
Lightning Source LLC
Chambersburg PA
CBHW032219190726
48289CB00007BA/2305